A Gecko's Dimension

I hope you enjoy this book. I am very happy to have you as a friend! See you in 2017!! :)

JL

Jennifer Lee

Printed in the U.S.A.
This title is available at Amazon online bookstore in North America and Europe and/or at other bookstores in Canada depending on the consignment condition.

ISBN: 978-1536987614

This book is dedicated to my mom and dad, who supported me so much in the journey of publishing my book

and to my lifetime mentor, *Sensei.*

CONTENTS

PART 1

ONE BIG JOURNEY, FOUR SMALL MINDS

PART 2

IN THE FLAMES OF REVENGE

PART 3

HEART RESTS AT HOME

"The important thing is to take that first step. Bravely overcoming one small fear gives you the courage to take on the next"

—Dr. Daisaku Ikeda

Part 1

ONE BIG JOURNEY, FOUR SMALL MINDS

chapter one

A NEW FRIEND

It is a fabulous late afternoon in May, with the leaves growing a light green over by the thick window glass, in the beautiful city of Langley. There is the tempting aroma of a crunchy cricket in the clear, fresh air.

I am a gecko, an eyelash crested gecko. I love eating crickets. My owners call me Max and that is my official name. I have a place that I call home. In my terrarium, there are lots of hiding places like the wooden hollow log and the green vine of smooth leaves. There is a water bowl and its sides are carved with careful hands to look like rocks. My food is a mango puree made from fine powder. I love to hunt nice crickets as I am doing now.

I look out of my little leafy peephole in the vines and wait for my food to get in my food bowl. Then Zap! I catch my prey in one strike. Thump, thump, thump! Go the feet of a cricket. I slowly crawl out of my hiding spot and gulp down the delicious snack.

I hear a noise. A-h-h-h! It is the water spray. I start to lick the water on the walls, leaves, and my face. Ouch! Some water lands in my eyes. I start to lick that off.

I have been jumping and catching crickets all night. It is around seven o'clock in the morning. I am exhausted, so I nestle in my little clear-glass cup to get some sleep.

I wake to the sound of the water spray. I know the owner lady usually mists my home around 7:00 p.m. Then a big hand reaches in and takes my empty food bowl. She comes back in a couple of hours with some brand new food. Yay! I gulp it all down with massive bites. Hours later in the early morning, I go to sleep again. But there is a strange noise like the sound of a ticking clock.

I wake up with a tired face and ask, "Who's there?"

There isn't an answer. Now I feel fed and pampered, but the sound comes again.

* * *

After a week of being pestered by the sound and having little sleep, I decide to find out who the culprit is, once and for all. Tonight I will stay up until 5:00 a.m. Well, I know a good way to keep myself awake. When I start to feel sleepy, I will dip my head into my water bowl. Then boom! I will be awake. Now I hide, waiting for the stranger.

I hear "tick, tick." Then I see a mouse, the size of a small butternut squash. I scream. In a second, the mouse turns around and squeaks in surprise. As he does, the mouse throws an object over his head and disappears.

The object falls through the space under the slightly open lid of my terrarium, where the water spray always comes through, and lands right on my head with a big clunk, making me jump onto the other side of the wall.

Seeing this, I do not want to go near the edge of my terrarium again. I also refuse to be taken out, but that is the place where my food and water is.

"What can I do? Do I have to starve?" I say to myself. "I'll get you back for this."

I then hang my head down in shame. I have never uttered such a mean word in my life.

It has been two days since I barely had a bite to eat or drink. But I am so famished that I cannot stand it anymore.

I cautiously climb the edge of the terrarium and take a small bite of food and a cautious lick of water. Then I gingerly go back to my hiding place, the hollow brown log.

* * *

A month has passed. I have totally forgotten about the existence of the mouse until I stumble upon a little blue tin heart. I can open and close it. I look at the heart and find an inscription carved in the center of the blue tin heart: *Willie the Mouse*.

"Huh!" I gasp.

Soon I think that the mouse might miss the heart, so I decide to give it back to him. However, I suddenly feel anxious. What would the mouse do to me? When I am about to change my mind about giving the heart back, Willie appears.

Willie smells of a stinky odor, and his deep-grey fur is covered in soot.

"Thank you for giving me the heart back. I was looking for it everywhere," Willie says.

We ask each other questions and start to get into a long conversation about our food, sleeping, families and homes.

Now I know that Willie loves to eat broccoli, sleeps in an empty tomato-sauce can near a dump, and has a sister named Wilma.

About half an hour later, Willie leaves for his home.

Behind-the-Scenes

(Favorite Foods of Max and his Friends)

1. Max's Special Mango Cake

This cake is the cake of the month. With its spongy and sweet feel and its delicate icing, this cake can really be tempting.

chapter two

THE STOLEN HEART

Several days have passed since Willie's visit. Surprisingly, my owner lady has decided to keep Willie as a house pet. She has got Willie some food and a cage unlike mine. The cage has a twisting neon-green slide and a small dark-purple hamster-wheel.

Since it is her job to feed both Willie and me, she takes out the bits of lumpy brown poop that Willie has left and neatens up my belongings in my terrarium. When we go to bed, we like to tell each other exotic tales from life. I feel curious and excited when I venture into my friend's stories in my dreams.

For a few days, I have been very contented until I hear a scream and a thud inside Willie's cage. I hear Willie's desperate voice: "My priceless blue tin heart is … STOLEN!"

"I'll never see that heart again," sobs Willie, filled with grief.

Trying to cheer him up, I say, "It's just a tin heart."

"You don't understand. That heart belonged to my great-great-great-grandfather. He treasured this heart more than ever, and he gave it to my great-great-grandfather who gave it to my great grandfather who…"

"Okay, okay, I get it!" I say. "So, what can we do?"

"We have to get it back!" screams frustrated Willie.

I search every corner and side of the terrarium. All night long, I hear Willie grumbling about how life is so unfair. I can understand him although the only bad thing that happened to me was when my owner family fed me apple sauce and some awful dried mealworms.

We search Willie's heart, but we cannot find it. However, we have found some clues which are a photo of a copy machine, some footprints, and a black top hat. We come down to two suspects—Willie's sister and one of my crickets. The cricket's name is Joey. He always wears a top hat similar to the one we found. We also suspect Willie's sister, Wilma because she always steals important things.

Willie gets out of his cage when night falls after he finds that the owner lady forgot to lock his cage after she fed him. Finally, Willie goes to the dump and asks his sister some questions, "Did you take my little blue tin heart that Great-great-great-grandpa gave me?"

"No," Wilma answers.

"One down one more to go," I say when Willie comes home in a tearful state, empty handed.

We have been still in shock since the heart was stolen. Now I witness Joey. Joey says he did not do anything but saw a dark-reddish-black bug sneak into Willie's cage and steal the blue tin heart. I feel a slight wave of hope when I hear this. I run off to tell Willie. When Willie hears the news, he leaps for joy.

"Wow, your cricket friend is real nice!" Willie says excitedly.

"Wait! How are we going to catch the thief when we don't know who the thief is?" I ask.

"Umm...," Willie mutters.

* * *

We are in trouble. BIG TIME. Most of all, we do not know where the thief lives and who the thief is. All day long, we whack our heads, trying to think about who stole the blue tin heart, and here are the results—nothing. Willie thinks that it might only take us a few days to find the criminal, but I do not think that is going to happen. We do not even have a hunch. We are still thinking what kind of bug it would be.

I finally find a solution and say, "It's probably the ants. I just know it!"

Willie nods in agreement and exclaims, "You are right."

The only question is where the ants have taken the heart. We decide to take a look at the clues again. During that time, we find scribbly handwriting at the back of the copy machine near my terrarium. The writing ends with the line saying "I will come again."

That last sentence makes Willie do a victory dance. I look at him in puzzled face.

"Don't you get it? We can spy on the thief!"

"Oh, that's why you're dancing like that!"

We are ready to spy. We both gather our spy gadgets that Willie brought from outside—a notebook, a pencil, and a pair of binoculars. We keep waiting until we finally hear a rustle, squeak, and beep near the old bookshelf.

"Aha," we both say, "we caught you red handed!"

"Sorry, but we did not steal anything. We have just passed by, but we might know who stole it for real—the beetles!" the ants exclaim.

An hour later, Willie fetches a beetle from the corner of his cage.

"Did you steal my blue tin heart?" Willie asks.

"No!" screams the terrified beetle.

Gulp! Willie eats the beetle.

We now ask a greedy grasshopper, a sick spider, and even a croaky cockroach, but we have no luck. All the way to the bed, Willie sobs—big, fat watery tears running down his chubby red cheeks.

Behind-the-Scenes

(Favorite Foods of Max and his Friends)

2. Willie's Cream-Cheese Poufs

These little blobs of deliciousness can have the power to lure you with the awesome experience of the cheese melting into a puddle right on your tongue.

chapter three

A JOURNEY INTO A NEW WORLD

It has been a while since Willie and I could not find any answer to our quest. I clearly see that his cheerful mind is fading. Last night, Willie was very sick. I cannot stand his sadness anymore.

When the night comes, I say to him, "Let's go find it."

"What?" Willie asks.

"The blue heart!" I exclaim.

I try to push out the terrarium glass, but it would not move. Willie tries to open his cage, too, but that does not work either.

Willie uses his tail to open his cage door. Luckily, his cage is not completely locked today. My owners sometimes forget to lock his cage. But my terrarium has a lid on top. The lid is usually closed, and a weight is placed on top to prevent me from escaping. After Willie comes out, he helps me to get out.

I remember something and say, "I know how we can go out. The door!"

"Okay," Willie says.

We both open up the latch and escape out into the darkness. We manage to slip out the front door of the house. We also take several useful items that we found inside the house—a wedge of cheese and an endless supply of gecko food, some broken rubber bands, a pile of leaves, and a big reference book for emergencies.

We venture up the world's most colossal boulders and immensely tall fences. Since this is the first time for me to come out of my home, I feel a tingling sensation in me. I just want to burst. The smell of the cherry blossoms swirls all around my joyful body in the fresh night-air. I am free!

The next day, we come across a river. It is a huge puddle. We cannot get across, so we just take the leaves to use as boats and find some twigs to use for paddles. We both paddle our way to the other side. Once we get there, we carry our boat rafts and go on our dangerous, terrifying, but hope-filled journey.

Later, we become worn out. We are very tired from carrying our boats and twig paddles. We lie down on some enormous rocks. I wonder if I would ever be able to see my owners again. I imagine how they would feel. Would they be upset? Would they be worried? At the thought of this, I suddenly feel a sense of sorrow and regret for what I have done.

* * *

It has been about a month since we left home. I am now getting homesick and sit down on a field to talk. Little did I know that the field is a school field. We both hear a sharp ring of a bell. We have to dodge kids' shoes, soccer balls, and rolling rocks. We dodge everything for about an hour. Also people scream because they are afraid of us.

"Eeek!" We hear one of the girls scream.

"Rat!" We hear one boy say in a quivery and shocked voice.

A teacher finally shoos Willie and me out. When we arrive at a quiet and shady place, we fall into a deep, happy sleep filled with snores.

I wake up and hear the rain patter on the ground. It is raining. Willie and I sigh.

"How will we find a shelter from the rain?" I ask Willie. "I don't want to have an uncomfortable sleep, with the rain falling on me."

"I don't either, but that's a really good question," Willie says deep in thought.

Finally he comes up with an idea and says, "We can gather sticks and some tree leaves to build a hut. We can also use some spruce gum and hay."

"That's a genius idea," I say enthusiastically.

We both start gathering bundles of spruce gum, sticks, leaves and branches from trees, and handfuls of hay.

Then we do some designing. We decide to make the roof out of leaves and hay. We are going to use the sticks to make walls, and we will use the spruce gum to stick everything together.

We start to build a hut. We plant the branches tightly and securely into the earth. We put some spruce gum on the sticks to glue them all together in one piece. Now we have a base. We then start to take the sticks to make a roof. We cover it with leaves and hay. We soon finish the small hut with a sturdy roof and a dirt floor.

We hear lightning and run inside. A while later, the vicious storm is gone, but we remember that we have left the canoes out in the rain.

I groan, "Oh well, we won't need them anyway."

Willie and I go back in, but suddenly, the hut shakes unbearably. The roof caves in. Half the stick door has fallen off. We run to see the devastation of our hut. We gasp in shock at the sight of our ruined hut. What used to be a hut is now in ruins. We stand in shock, with the rain pouring buckets on us.

We waste no time and run to the nearest bush, panting. We grab branches with leaves on them and hold them over our heads for makeshift umbrellas. We need a plan—a good one—of course. Finally, an idea pops into my mind.

"We could use those sturdy grape vines over there to fix our mistakes like the door and roof," I suggest.

I point to the vines over in the garden.

"That's a good idea," Willie says.

We run to the patch of grape vines in the garden, with our umbrellas waving. When we get there, we are drenched in fresh raindrops. We start to pick the grape vines with the juiciest grapes on them, and we run back.

We gather the grapes and put them down on the grass. We thread the broken part of the bottom of the hut with the grape vines. We go to the top and fix the door. We secure the hinges to the hut and double-knot the door. We now decide to make a small stick-fence so the crows cannot peck down our hut.

We go inside of the small hut and nestle in a loft of hay.

"Tomorrow, we will find your blue tin heart," I promise to Willie.

Behind-the-Scenes

(Favorite Foods of Max and his Friends)

3. Max's Cricket Carrot-Cake

This is the best bug cake in the bakery!

chapter four

THE MYSTERIOUS COBRA

The next morning, I pull Willie off a loft of hay to play. We play catch with a blue marble that I have found on the green field. We also play soccer with one of our leftover mud-balls. We weave hats out of hay and make sandals.

We lie down on the grass and look at the fluffy-pillow white clouds. We see an image of a gecko and a mouse wearing sparkling golden hats and shoes. We also see an image of a train and finally a mud soccer ball like the one I have played with.

When we go back to the hut, we see a beautiful swallow with soft feathers lying down on the ground. Willie and I feel quite sorry for the bird and carry the bird inside the hut. We both start collecting leaves so we can cover the bird for warmth.

"Why don't we let this bird live in here? We need to leave anyway," I suggest.

"You're right. After she wakes up, she may like this hut," Willie adds.

* * *

We set off back on track. We walk until we can walk no more. As soon as we come to a clearing, we take a rest. I guess that we have walked too far.

We find ourselves in a deep forest. It is raining, and we helplessly settle down on the soaking wet grass. We stand up, dripping from resting in the rain. Suddenly, an extremely bright white flash of light appears in front of our petrified faces—the king cobra!

"You horrible thing step away and go back to the lonely place you came from!" Willie stammers.

The snake wraps his dark-red tail against his flesh and forms a magical blue light which sparkles like the frost on a leaf in winter. Then he reveals a small blue tin heart in the center of the dazzling light. It is Willie's heart. I can see

Willie in the corner of my eye. His mouth is trembling.

"Give me the blue heart back," Willie says with all the courage he can muster.

"How foolish you are to think that I would give it back to you," the cobra cackles.

The cobra rubs his tail again, and Willie is thrown off his feet onto the hard ground. The cobra rubs his tail a third time, and one by one, fiery big red letters are pulled out of his long twisted body.

One of the letters says:

Go up north to succeed. You will find some vines to lead.
P.S.: You have to bring Moon Girl to me.

The flames lick the air as if they were feeding. A couple of seconds later, the cobra fades into thin air. I write the riddle down in my notebook.

We head for the north. I carry my orange backpack filled with useful utensils on my shoulders.

Behind-the-Scenes

(Favorite Foods of Max and his Friends)

4. Max's Cricket Mousse

This mousse has all good flavor, soft texture, and the most satisfying crunch in every bite.

chapter five

THE MOON GIRL

We walk and follow the trees and logs with the most moss. We continue until we reach a grove of vines. Once we get there, Willie's nose starts to quiver.

"I feel something coming," Willie remarks.

Suddenly a vine comes, shooting at us. We dodge it just in time, but another comes, wrapping me in its grasp.

"Lead the vines like the riddle says," I manage to choke out.

Willie tugs the vine off of me. We both find sticks and

use them as swords. After a while, the vines open, leading us to a tower just like the one the cobra has shown us.

It is made out of remarkably glossy wood that shimmers like the stars in the moody white moonlight. At the top, there is a shining diamond secured in a clear case.

There is a door that is concealed by a tall statue of the Moon Girl. We push away the statue and knock twice on the door.

When there is a huge bright flash, we both close our eyes as tightly as we can. A minute later, we find ourselves facing a beautiful girl.

She has light blond hair and wears a white silk dress that shimmers in the light. She also wears a moon-shaped pendant that is covered in silver sparkles. Her pants have little specks of moon dust shaped and painted to look like planets. Even her eyes are space blue.

She asks, "Why are you here?"

"My friend's blue tin heart has disappeared. It was a gift from his great-great-great-grandfather. We've been trying to find it. On the way to find the heart, we met a cobra. He said he had stolen it, and the only way for us to get it back is that we would have to give you to him."

"Sorry, I can't do that, but I can lead you to someone who can help you to get the heart back."

"Who is here?" I ask.

The girl does not answer. Instead, she gives me a scroll. It says:

Walk the path and stomp on the ground.
Wait until you hear a bird of a magical world.
Follow the bird, named Ally, to the diamond river.
Please do run, or you shall shiver.
Look for a mountain that was once one's only hope.
Then go to a patch with a little slope.
You have reached your destination.
Hip, hip, hooray!
Now look for a squire of a horse with a golden mane.
Please for whatever you do, don't laugh or giggle.
If you do, you shall perish.

Willie and I read the riddle, and I say, "Okay, let's stomp our feet on the ground to call for a bird."

We do so. A cute little bird appears out of the ground. She looks almost magical with beautiful crystal-blue wings and majestic deep-black eyes. She is Ally.

She leads us under the ground into the earth, and we walk until we finally come to the diamond river.

It has a diamond bridge. I see the water. It is as white

as quartz, and light purple lilacs are growing around the jade-green bank. It is a beautiful sight.

Behind-the-Scenes

(Favorite Foods of Max and his Friends)

5. Moon Girl's Star Meringues

These meringues are the best meringues in the century. You could really say that they are quite stars!

chapter six

THE FAIRY CAFE

I hear some humming and see two beautiful fairies, each one with crystal blue hair and eyes. A leaf appears in my hands.

It reads: *"You are meeting the Diamond-River fairies!"*

"Hello," sings a tall fairy, "my name is Crystal, and this is my sister Crystalin."

"What brings you to the diamond river?" she asks, beckoning to the sparkling water right behind her.

"We are just passing by," I say with a slight scowl.

Crystalin whispers something to Crystal. The only

words I hear are "they're…stuck…to…feet." After that, the fairies giggle for a long time and start to laugh.

"Ha-ha-ha!"

"You may pass," Crystalin says, still laughing.

"Thank you," Willie and I respond and start to leave in confusion.

We now discover that we have been tricked by the fairies and stuck right in the center of the diamond bridge.

"Hey," I bark.

"You will be our slaves forever!" the fairies cackle.

The fairies leave to have lunch. Although Willie and I are stuck, the bird is still free. She melts the ice by pumping her crystal blue wings.

We start to feel hungry. I can hear my stomach rumbling. Then I smell some worm meatloaf, cricket carrot cake with extra-large cricket sprinkles, and a sugary-sweet yellow mango pastry made out of the finest gecko powder mixture in the whole country. I wonder if I am hallucinating. There is also an unfamiliar smell. Willie also gasps and jumps up and down.

"Chee-e-se!" I can hear Willie mumbling.

We continue to walk until we forget how far we have walked. At the end of the trail, we find a shabby little cottage with a sign that says: *"Welcome to the Fairy Cafe."*

I ask Willie if we can eat something here.

Willie nods and smiles happily.

As soon as we go through the front door, we become highly amazed. The inside of the shabby little cottage is now a luxurious house with a shatter-free glass window overlooking the panorama of the beautiful breezy sea.

Willie asks, "How are we going to buy food when we have no money?"

"Fortunately, I brought my checkbook just in case for us," the bird says.

"Great," I cheer.

I order a crunchy mealworm meatloaf, a cricket carrot cake with extra-large cricket sprinkles, and a poufy mango pastry. The food is so delicious and we dine like kings. After we eat, we pay and start on the other trail.

"How was that Fairy Cafe?"

"Well, I guess I ate way too much food. The next thing I know is that my stomach is the size of a water melon," Willie exaggerates.

I can see obviously that Willie's is much bigger. Willie now starts to brag about how much bigger his stomach is compared to mine. I cannot take it any longer.

"THIS IS NOT A CONTEST FOR ANIMALS WITH BIG STOMACHS!" I scream in anger.

A wave of silence falls over us. I feel devastated and begin to think dark thoughts, thoughts that have never come out since long ago when my owners fed me apple sauce. I wonder why I have become friends with Willie in the first place. Well, if I were at home, I could be fed crickets, be held and washed.

"I'm so sorry," Willie utters the words barely audible.

Meanwhile, the bird is looking a bit scared. But after I hear Willie's apology, my anger slowly calms down.

"I forgive you," I say to Willie.

It is now 1:00 a.m. I sense that a storm will be coming in this bleak weather. The bird, Willie, and I huddle together in a pile of leaves and fall into a deep sleep.

Behind-the-Scenes

(Favorite Foods of Max and his Friends)

6. Sunflower-Seed Muffins

These are all the rage in Ally's flock. You can't get away with even one savory treat!

chapter seven

FINDING THUMB MOUNTAIN

Ally looks up at the sky. Home is the word she treasures the most out of all the words she likes, the word that carries many meanings. The word "home" means her family—her brothers Auzy and Jonathan, her mother Allison, her father Adam, and her uncle John, along with her aunty Jenny. She misses all of them, every single one of her family and relatives.

Ally uses her favorite crystal pen and writes:

"Find Thumb Mountain far north and start climbing to find a steep edge."

Then she sets off for her home far in the sky. She is small but is also mighty against the rough, high storms.

My hand brushes across a piece of paper, and I read the note written by Ally, the silver bird.

Willie says, "I saw a thumb-shaped mountain in the distance. It is covered with ornate flowers and vines. The top is slanted and peaked to look like a thumb."

We pack our things and set off. We walk. We skip. We run and sprint. Hours later, we come to the bottom of the majestic mountain standing thirty feet tall and having a unique thumb-shaped peak.

We start to climb the gigantic mountain. The trail is covered with bones and fossilized animal skulls. Willie gives me a boost onto the second ledge. Some ledges are big enough to sit on, but others are crumbling right at our feet.

We manage to make it about ten feet in the air before Willie freaks out. Unfortunately, he has a fear of heights. I tell him to take a seat. We find a ledge big enough and thick enough for both of us to curl up on.

"We need to make a plan," I suggest.

Willie is not listening.

"Take a deep breath, Willie!" I encourage him, gripping on tight to his shoulders.

Suddenly, we fall. Willie snaps out of his trance and quickly holds onto the pieces of rock that jut out from the mountain. A little hermit crab finds us hanging from the rough pieces of rock.

"Stop screaming, you're hurting my ears!" the hermit crab says, obviously irritated.

"Hello, we need some help here!" I ask with an eye roll.

"Okay," the crab replies.

He leaves and does not seem to come back, leaving us hanging until we die. When I seriously feel that I am going to fall, I see the hermit crab coming back with a ladder. He helps us get down. When Willie finally reaches the ground, he kisses the grainy sand with joy.

The crab takes us to his hotel. It is filled with luxurious items. We eat dinner at a fancy Italian restaurant and play checkers. Then we go to bed.

As I pull the covers up to my chin, I ask Willie, "When are we going home?"

"I don't know," Willie responds. "Well, we better figure out."

I manage just before I drift off. We have just been served eggs and bacon for breakfast. We get some relaxation in a Jacuzzi. A little later, we play tennis and reluctantly sip terribly sour lemonade.

The next day, we say good-bye to the hermit crab and go back onto the mountain. We keep on climbing and arrive at a really steep edge. I gasp. I start creeping quietly towards the safe cover of the trees.

Behind-the-Scenes

(Favorite Foods of Max and his Friends)

7. Bird-Seed Spaghetti

Savory hot noodles tossed with all types of birdseeds. They are the perfect surprise dinner on a cold rainy day.

chapter eight

THE GOLDEN STABLE

Willie and I climb the mountain. We encounter many interesting sights like the dark-green putting of Goblin Golf Course, the decorative carpet from Diddly Dwarf's Doormat Repairs, the shining-red fruit-drooping from the ends of the branches of the trees at the orchards in the Fairy Cherry Farm, and the fancy dance-floor in Robin Hood Restaurant.

We arrive at the stable for the golden horse. We sneak towards the barn and get a good look at it. It has a golden door and fresh new planks of wood nailed together to make the walls. We wait for the squire to take out the horse to feed him or give him exercise. We wait for him to do anything else just to make the horse come out.

We hear the ticking noise of the squire's watch. I hide with Willie behind a tree. The squire is a chubby small young man. His name is Quincy. He is wearing a too tight business suit with a grubby-green checkered tie. His stable boy is wearing a simple pair of worn jeans and navy-blue overalls.

We wait until they leave. I gingerly tiptoe through the hay-covered ground and release the golden horse. His mane is glittery, soft and is the color of gold. His eyes are a soft yellow-brown. His hoofs are as black as ebony and as shiny and smooth as black pearl. He is quite small for his kind.

We find no place to sleep here. We decide to rest on the horse. The horse's back is surprisingly like a fluffy pillow. Apparently, it is the softest makeshift mattress ever.

I wake up to the sound of Willie yawning. Willie has just woken up, too. At first, we are very puzzled about why we are on this magnificent horse. Then we remember why and keep on riding. On the way, we find a pile of hard brown wood. We get off the horse and pick up the pieces of wood since I have an idea.

"Let's build a small wagon for us to put behind the horse so he can pull us," I suggest.

Now we smear all the pieces of wood with brown gooey mud and construct our wagon. We wait for it to dry. When it is done, we go to sleep on the long wavy-green grass.

When I check the mud the next morning, it is totally dry. We braided some grass the other night to make reins. Willie eats a handful of berries and I eat gecko food. We both pack our things. I pack some food, water, and a notepad. Willie brings a jug full of water, a new boat, and some berries.

Before we leave, we go to a nearby pond. Inside the pond, we find male bullfrogs. For quite a while, we watch the bullfrogs jump and croak and dive.

I ask Willie if he would like to climb a tree with me to pick some apples. Willie agrees. I go first swiftly climbing the tree's limb. Willie is not too bad himself. He can get a decent leap, but later he almost faints. I quickly stop Willie, who is panting. I climb towards the top of the tree.

"Ally is in the tree!" I shout to Willie.

We both climb up the tree as fast as we can move. I grab Ally's feathers and pull. I ask Willie to go down and make a soft landing for Ally to fall on. Willie makes a cushion out of leaves. I drop Ally. The hard landing snaps Ally into control. I get down. She thanks us and we all hug.

Ally tells us about her journey home:

She reached the middle of the Pacific Ocean. For some reason, she felt very nervous. She tried to take a deep breath, but immediately she lost balance. When she looked down, she started falling and falling fast.

"Help!" Ally screamed. She closed her eyes and braced for impact.

While shouting, she felt herself being lifted into the air and then transported onto the ground.

She looked up, straightened from her flattened position. She saw a bird with sparkly black hair and pearly white tail feathers. Her body was covered in gold and silver sparkles.

"H-h-hello!" Ally stammered.

"I'm Melinda."

They got up. Melinda took Ally's hand. They walked and chatted each other until they came to a stop in the front of a bakery. Ally smelled doughnuts, chocolate cakes filled with cherry jam and various types of flavors of cake. Ally walked inside of the bakery. She smelled roses and saw a variety of bakery treats set out just for her. Melinda offered her a comfortable blue mat to sleep on with a pattern of stars on it. Ally accepted.

After eating, Ally said goodbye to Melinda and set off. Ally finally became exhausted after she reached the apple tree we were passing by. Fortunately, she was found by us.

We go back on our scary but quite exciting journey again.

Behind-the-Scenes

(Favorite Foods of Max and his Friends)

8. Bakery-Baked Brownies

These have been a great improvement on horse meals. They are much thicker than slop but tastier than bread!

chapter nine

THE COBRA'S SECRET BUSH

Our horse-carriage wagon passes by many unfamiliar places. On the way, the cobra is waiting for us.

Hisssssss! The cobra is blowing fire out of his nose in anger.

"I will not let those wimpy creatures take my blue heart. Mine. Yes, mine!" he proclaims with such arrogance.

Smoke is coming out of his ears, nostrils, and mouth. The cobra decides to see what his enemies are doing. He creates a ball made out of pure magic. It lights up the secret bush. A combined image of a gecko, mouse, bird, and golden-shimmery horse appears in the crystal light ball. At first the image is a bit blurry, but now the image is clearly visible. We see the cobra going to his lair.

I am riding in the wagon behind the horse. The horse is carrying passengers and supplies such as a notebook, some food, broken rubber bands, and a pile of crunchy leaves.

"So, they've got partners," the cobra blurts with smirk.

Suddenly, he remembers an old saying that his dear grandmother used to tell him:

"Use magic wisely. Don't lose your temper. But remember one thing: always have fun."

At that moment, the smoke comes out of his ears and nostrils even harder. He finds a clue.

Rumble. Rumble. Rumble. The ground shakes. The shaking surprises me. We have been riding in this wagon led by the horse for five hours, and we really want to get to the cobra's secret bush by the time the sun sets. I have heard that it is horrifying and concealed by dark magic, with full of bugs. I am hoping there will be crickets.

Suddenly, the rumbling stops, and standing in front of

us is the cobra. He has used a magic potion by blending ten eye balls, two toad feet, a pixie-dog's poop, and dragon dust. He has mixed them all in a black cauldron that was heated by the fire. He pours the potion into a small green bottle and sprinkles it over his head.

After I hear a bam, a flash, and a click, he is shrunken into the size of an ant. He uses all his tiny muscles to slither up the gigantic cauldron and lands on a comfy, soft cloud.

"WHAT! THEY ARE SUPPOSED TO BE MISERABLE!" the cobra squeaks.

I have just seen the ant-sized cobra come in front of the wagon. I look at Willie, who looks very scared.

"What's the matter?" I ask in my gentlest voice.

"T-h-e b-b-blue h-h-heart! I tried to grab it, but it disappeared. It started to grow into a puzzle piece. I tried again and again, but nothing worked. The puzzle pieces fit altogether, and the puzzle showed the cobra on it," Willie says.

"It looks like the cobra is up to his old tricks again," I say.

The whole cobra puzzle piece thing makes me think that we should take some revenge onto that mean, witchy old cobra.

The next morning, I shake Willie to wake him up so that I can tell him about my idea for revenge, but Willie does not wake up. I try a few more times, but then I give up. I am so mad and tired.

"Oh, why doesn't anyone help me?" I ask the thin air in front of my face.

I go over to Ally to see if she is awake and can help me. Ally is usually an early bird, but today she is kind of being lazy.

"Well, I have a lot of patience, so I'll wait till she wakes up from her sleep," I say to myself.

I wait and wait until I finally am about to burst. Now I give up and walk away. I am trying to come up with some ideas, so I think and think. Finally, I got an idea. I cannot wait any longer. I have to tell them my brilliant idea.

I scream, "I HAVE AN IDEA!"

They all wake up and I tell my idea.

When I tell them my plan, they call me a genius. I will climb with my friends to the top of the distant mountain, which holds a beautiful magical garden with a statue made out of pure gold. This is where the cobra lives. I will steal the blue heart and go off with it. That is my plan.

As soon as we arrive at the mountain, I sneak up to the bushes with Willie, Ally, and Alvin the Horse. When we see the most breathtaking sight, a huge cauldron covered in poisonous grape vines in a big shelf which stores many potions in vials, we also see the heart. We have to get it.

* * *

Now, everybody knows that getting the heart back will not be easy, but we have to try. I put the huge pile of wood on the ground. The heart is high up, so we decide to make an animal ladder with me on top. Alvin goes on the top of the pile of wood and kneels to let Willie, Ally, and me on.

I grab the heart. We run out with the heart before anyone can notice. Willie cannot stop jumping up and down. We have gotten the heart back. We are all filled with glee. I am so happy that I do not notice any danger around me.

We have gotten Willie's beautiful blue tin heart back. The best part is that we now realize that the clear blue heart has magic power since we saw the cobra use it, but we do not know how to use it and even what it is about.

I am just as happy and free as the leaves rustling through the wind. My mind is blowing with wonderful, glorious, and fantastic thoughts of all kinds.

I feel like flying, watching all the beautiful birds

around me. Letting the wind settle down onto my face, I see the panorama picture and the azure blue water.

They seem to be all set up around me.

Behind-the-Scenes

(Favorite Foods of Max and his Friends)

9. Cheese Icecream

This is a mouse favorite. With its rich taste of cheese and low sugar rates, this will be the best food for mice in all the land!

chapter ten

WILLIE'S DISAPPEARANCE

I feel a tingling sensation in my body again. Two beams of beautiful and silly imagination run through from my tiny toes to my overflowing brain. I feel as if I placed a light bulb right above me, and it were just switched on.

"I got it," I say to himself.

The flying daydream has given me the best idea ever in my life.

I say, "We can just fly home!"

"How?" Willie asks.

I suggest, "We can build an airplane."

We start to draw out a plan of how we can build the plane on a leaf. It looks magnificent. I look closely at the drawing. It has layers and layers of sticks for the wings attached by hay and blobs of mud. The body of the plane is made out of about fifty layers of hay knotted together. On the top is a huge number of sticks smudged with globs of mud. For the wheels, we will sculpt mud to look like circles with holes and put them on the bottom.

We get to work. I collect the supplies while Willie makes sure that everything is good and stuck together. Ally puts the roof on by flying up and putting it on the plane.

When the plane is done, Alvin jumps on it to make sure it is sturdy enough. We have done it. The moment we decide to take a break, however, I hear a voice familiar to me.

A-a-h-h! I—Vanessa, the evil apprentice of the King Cobra—yawn just at dawn. The sun casts above my fort, which holds vials of poison that includes pixie eyes, dragon dust, and the most important ingredient: my power.

The cobra has changed ever since he was a child. The world was very different from today. The sky had an eerie glow of darkness that spread everywhere.

One day, a very special day, a boy witch was born from a mother witch that longed to be good. The mother was very young, judging by her size. She stood only a few feet tall. Her family also loved her to the tips of their warty crooked noses. It was her son who loved her most.

But the father died when the son became only eighteen months. After that, the mother's boss cursed her son to become a cobra, still capable of magic.

The cobra moved out of his home with agony piercing his heart. He went to a cottage near the forest, living with a vicious lady. As he stayed in the cottage, he learned to be bad.

Years and years passed to this very day, and he solemnly declared himself an evil witch. He slithered off to a cave filled with dark magic. He has come to steal the blue tin heart. But he has lost the opportunity… FOR NOW. We do not notice what kind of evil trick he is planning, ONCE AND FOR ALL.

I wake up to find the sky darker than normal. Instead of the birds' chirping, I hear the howl of the distant wolves.

"Well, it's gloomier than usual," I say expecting an

answer.

Willie stays silent. I wait until he has an answer. It doesn't come. At first, I think he is playing a trick on me. But then I look to the side—Willie is gone.

We are all shocked and do not know what to do. But I determine to find Willie and say, "We're leaving."

"B-B-B-u-t," Ally stammers.

"I also vote for finding Willie," Alvin announces.

"Fine," Ally agrees hesitantly.

We pack all our belongings and set off. We head for the cobra's secret bush again, knowing that we would be the only ones who have the nerve to kidnap Willie.

We come to the distant mountain only to find that we have to climb it and move a gigantic boulder that is blocking the first ledge. We all try to push it out of the way, but that is not going to happen even after we try hard.

We get a brilliant idea. Alvin goes right next to the boulder. I go on top of him and Ally goes on the very top. Ally jumps up onto the uncovered ledge that is resting right on top of the boulder and I climb up with her. Then Alvin jumps on with us, too.

We have done it. We keep on going back and forth around the mountain. There is no trace of Willie. We keep on climbing until we come to a clearing. We push some rocks behind, and nobody would believe what we have just seen—the cobra's bush.

Now, all we have to do is to find Willie. Where can we find him? Also, there is one big question—how? We whack our heads, trying to find an idea. Still we cannot find one.

We keep on trying to think of an idea but it would not come. We try to call for help but no one comes. It is time for us to take matters in our own hands.

Ally tells us, "I have an idea. Since the cobra is evil, he should be keeping Willie up north. All we have to do is to follow the trees with the most moss."

I think that is a genius idea. We both take the long grass from a patch near a stump and braid it to make a giant rope. We take fallen leaves and secure them with knots from some longer grass to make a grass belt. Then we go from tree to tree looking for moss.

We decide to take a small break. I cut off some pine needles that still have some nectar on them. We take some of them and put them in my water to make a fresh drink. I use the leftovers and share them with my two friends.

We eat our snacks, chewing thoughtfully.

"You know, if we want to collect moss, we should. Moss is a very powerful healing aid," I remark.

"Cool!" Alvin exclaims.

We all eagerly start running from tree to tree to find the moss. I have found approximately sixteen ounces of moss and Ally has collected thirty ounces. Alvin only has collected ten ounces. Altogether we have collected fifty-six ounces of moss.

Collecting the moss also helps us get closer to where the cobra is holding Willie captive. I feel anxious about the idea that we should save Willie on our own.

Behind-the-Scenes

(Favorite Foods of Max and his Friends)

10. Mealworm Salad

This salad consists of all sorts of creepy crawlies including crickets. Serve it with mango juice and calcium powder for the best results!

Behind-the-Scenes

(Favorite Foods of Max and his Friends)

11. Oats and Macaroni

This is not your regular macaroni-and-cheese. This is a horse favorite. This dish really qualifies as comfort food.

chapter eleven

AN UNEXPECTED ATTACK

I can imagine how Willie would feel now. I can clearly see him sigh. He has been stuck in a tiny cell for longer than he expected. I know that the walls are hard and creepy and the front of the cell is sealed with iron bars. There are barely enough cracks to see the barren world outside.

Willie might miss the times when he could be fed and have a clean home. But since the time he went searching for his blue tin heart, he has lost even that comfort. Now he also has lost something more important—*friends*. He may wonder if I am trying to rescue him or not.

We take a rest so we can be ready to face the cobra. After that, we eat and jog around the green forest. By the time we get there, my throat feels like sandpaper and my eyes become red and itchy. I wonder what the cobra has done to Willie. What if it is too late? What if the cobra has done something bad to him? I shudder at the thought.

"Are you okay?" Ally asks.

"Yes," I answer, with my voice hoarse.

Willie snores. He always snores a lot especially when he is very tired, but today he hears a sound that snaps him into control. He huddles against the wall, not daring to make a sound. It must be the cobra—he thinks.

All of a sudden, the sound comes closer. Willie closes his eyes, waiting for his tragic ending. He feels a nudge. This is it—he thinks. A familiar voice makes him sit up.

"Max, how did you get here?" Willie asks quite frazzled.

"It's not only me. It's all of us." I answer.

Ally gives Willie his blue tin heart back with her beak raised high.

"My blue tin heart!" Willie exclaims.

We all hug.

Once we get back to the woods, I ask Ally and Alvin

where they would be staying after Willie and I return home. Willie and I pack our things. We board the plane and test the tin heart for some magic force to motorize the plane.

"Bye, Alvin. Bye, Ally," Willie and I both greet.

I substitute as pilot.

"Remember, Max, steer left to go right and steer right to go left."

"I remember, Ally," I exclaim with confidence, and we set off.

After a few hours of our flight, we feel a sudden wind coming from the west then from the east. The earth below rumbles from time to time. Willie clutches the blue tin heart as tightly as he dares with his furry hands. After a brief wind falls over, silence fills the air.

A slippery and sharp tongue grabs the heart with a force that would turn the plane over if I did not shake it off. We are falling and the heart is gone.

My hands freeze in shock. I realize what Willie and I have done. We have just risked our lives to get the heart back that can only be endured by a strong bond. We may have to repeat the whole thing to get the heart back, once and for all. But even if the heart is gone, the bond of friendship will still be there forever.

Behind-the-Scenes

(Magic Potions and Drinks by the Cobra)

1. The Love Potion

The Cobra's love potion is an enchanting love maker that enjoins two people's hearts.

Part 2
IN THE FLAMES OF REVENGE

chapter twelve
A NEW BEGINNING

Plink, plink, plink. The rain splatters on the glass that is shattered on the bare ground. The streets are coated in a fresh powdery layer of snow that is now slowly melting, reminding me of my loneliness. Two flags attached to the poles read: WELCOME TO VANCOUVER. None of my friends are here—just me. I am all alone.

I wonder how Willie is doing. Would he feel as lonely as I am? It's freezing here, so freezing that half my tail is frostbitten.

I don't really know if I can take it any longer. I sit and

wait for the sun to go down as my stomach growls in protest. I am very hungry. I wonder if Ally is hungry or maybe Alvin. I don't really know if Ally would be hungry with such a small appetite.

But Alvin is probably hungry. I can just imagine him moping beneath the trees, with his belly rumbling like a stampede of bison. Poor Alvin! I bet he is searching for food in desperation right now.

What about Willie? What if he is starving and tired, too? I just hate the situation that we are in. How could this happen to us? We are not bad people, I mean, bad animals. I wonder when we will find one another. I guess only time will tell.

I wake up at the crack of dawn. When the sun just comes up, I walk north and come to a pool of water. How is this pool not frozen? This place has no trees, houses, or civilization but just bare white snow.

The wind blows in my face. I am cold and miserable. But I am very curious about how Willie, Ally, and Alvin are doing.

I walk over to a grassy ditch filled with fluffy, sparkling white snow up to the rim and decide to build an igloo out of the snow that surrounds me. I carefully shape clumps of snow into neat, satisfactory bricks.

I repeat this step about a thousand times. Then I stack up the ice bricks in a circular pattern. About a million years later, I am finally done.

The result is not so good, but it provides fine shelter and surprisingly good warmth. The size of the igloo is not very big. It would only fit about two people. But it is perfectly fine for now.

I cover the ground in fresh well-patted snow, creating a soft but solid, sturdy ground. Just to make sure that there will be extra thick walls, I slowly pat some snow in the holes and cracks on the snowy wall.

I do another layer. I keep on doing this until the walls are crack-free.

Now I punch a hole in the front of the igloo no bigger than half a sheet of blank paper and get to work on my frostbitten tail. I find a piece of paper and wrap it right around my tail. I jump up and down to bring back my warmth. But it is no use.

I decide to make a blanket with some sheets of paper I have found on the snow-covered ground. I stack them to create a sheer paper blanket.

I make another one to use as a makeshift carpet. Ah, it is much warmer!

I drape the blanket over my shivering shoulders. It

does not feel as warm as a normal blanket but feels much better than nothing at all. I go deeper into the snow.

Before, I had no idea about how scary it would in the wilderness. I hear the wind screeching outside. I hear multiple sounds of wild animals making creepy noises in the distance. I shiver up into a tight ball.

If I could sweat, I would sweat like crazy. But too bad, I am a reptile. Reptilian species don't sweat. In other words, I am truly terrified.

Soon, two big hands pick me up. I sit in a large plastic container, trying to push my way out. There is a silence that ends with a very sudden plunk. After that, it is pitch black and darkness swarms in my eyes. I begin to see stars, and then I pass out.

When I wake up, two humans are scribbling notes on paper held by clipboards. I close my eyes and turn around to the scratchy mattress. Everybody leaves now.

My stomach is the only thing that makes a sound in the entire glass-walled room. I begin to hear footsteps. I wince, wondering if it is the people again. Instead, there is a nice-looking lady pushing a cart with Willie and Ally on it.

I almost fall off the bed in surprise. I do not know how this can happen. Maybe they knew how lonely I was and appeared to me, or maybe I'm hallucinating. Well, I don't care as long as my friends are back.

The lady sets down the cart and carefully puts Willie and Ally towards me. I press on the plastic wall, wanting so badly to get out of this little prison.

There is a little click and Ally, Willie, and I are all trapped in one enormous tank. We all groan. I think how things can get worse than this.

One by one, the most horrible things happen. The lady who captured us brings another guest. I can't believe how it can happen, but it does. Another prisoner in a different tank is … the cobra.

I can't believe my eyes. The cobra is the thief who stole Willie's precious blue heart. I tap Willie on the back, and as soon as he knows what is going on, he staggers back into the corner.

Behind-the-Scenes

(Magic Potions and Drinks by the Cobra)

2. The Evil Potion

The Cobra really knows how to get the mischievous gland out of you. He uses his evil potion!

Behind-the-Scenes

(Magic Potions and Drinks by the Cobra)

3. The Peter's Brew Potion

The Peter's Brew Potion turns you into a lost boy. Recommended by Tinkerbell!

chapter thirteen

WILLIE'S STORY

Willie was hiding behind the Moon Girl's castle all along. He was saved by the Moon Girl after he fell in the ocean from the plane. He was about to drift off when she woke him up.

She directed him to go to the mountain and nowhere else. She said if he went anywhere else, he would meet the cobra and his doom. He shivered.

Although the Moon Girl had told him to heed her instructions, he went right ahead to search for Max. Willie made a wrong choice by going to find him. On the way, Willie met an old lady with a hunched back. She pointed at him with an icy hand.

"You-you-you!" she muttered and left in a burst of sparkles.

Willie ran as fast as he could. He dodged tress and skittered past fallen branches. He bumped into a gigantic lady. The even worse part was that she had the cobra in her arms.

Willie screamed. The lady picked him up towards the cobra's mouth. Willie closed his eyes and waited for his life to end.

Then Ally swooped in and picked him up with her talons. Willie felt as if he could reach the sky and soared through effortlessly, cutting through clouds and other birds. They flew until they bonked into a gigantic net.

Willie screamed in Ally's face. They were taken down, down, down as if it would never end. Finally, they were placed on a cart pushed by a burly big, tall lady and transported to a building called Vancouver Animal Control Centre.

Ally and Willie both winced in fright. They squirmed. They wiggled. They were quite desperate to get free.

Willie finishes his story off with a heave of his shoulders and a frustrated sigh.

Here we are now, lost and scared. We glare at each

other. I stare at the bare walls, my tail shaking with terror.

I go to the walls of the container and bang against it with my head.

"There must be some way out," I say to myself.

Ally beats at the wall with her wings and Willie slumps. After a while, I just give up.

"Maybe we have to live here forever," I complain to Allie and Willie.

It is one o'clock in the morning, and we are in silence. I fall into an endless, dreamless sleep. So do Willie and Ally.

I wake up to find an avalanche of snow falling straight down on the container and one tiny unexpected guest inside our tank.

"Ohhh," I heave a deep sigh.

My friends wake up, and they also have worries to think about. We walk around the container a few times and another few times.

When we hear a bizarre noise, a peculiar creature with whiskers and the silkiest ears comes out. It has paws and claws. I think I have seen my owners fuss about this before.

"Ally, Willie," I introduce, "please warmly welcome our new friend, Mittens."

"Huh?" they both wonder.

"Mittens," I repeat the new friend's name.

chapter fourteen

MITTENS THE CAT

At first sight, Willie and Ally are scared and shocked. But the calm, sensitive behavior of Mittens seems to put Ally at ease.

"He'll eat me. I'm sure," Willie blurts out his worries after spending half an hour in the corner, with his head down.

"Mittens eats flesh?" Ally doubts with a laugh.

"Willie, that will never happen," I reassure him.

I sit against the wall in the slightly foggy big container, in boredom. Mittens is prowling around the container. He sees something with two gigantic holes in it. The humans outside call it a cat apartment. A cat can go up and down in the cat apartment, crawling from top to bottom and back from bottom to top.

After watching Mittens go back and forth for what seems like an hour, I go and see what Ally and Willie are doing. Willie is pacing frantically up, down, and around the container. Ally is making sure the cobra doesn't come close to our container.

I ask if they want to help me make a plan to find Alvin.

"Sure," they both reply with bright smiles spreading on their faces.

I smile back at both of them. Suddenly, Mittens wails as the lady from the place puts him in what is apparently called a kitty crate.

When the lady releases us from our plastic prison to transfer us to another tank, we narrowly escape, unnoticed, and secretly slip into the cat crate. Inside, we meet Mittens. His tail works as a big fluffy couch for us to sit on. We sit and our hands are frozen by our sides. Then the crate goes up into an automobile. I have once been in one like this before—it is a car.

The car jerks and pushes forward in an amazingly fast

burst of speed. The only sound I hear is the wind whipping vigorously in my ear holes. I also hear the scuffles of his sharp intact claws. I crawl over to the cat's leg and lean my head against it. The soft purr of the cat lures me into a peaceful, comfortable sleep.

When I wake up, the wind has stopped and so has the car. We stop in front of a building that is made out of white concrete bricks.

The big sign on the wall reads: Dr. Nelson's Pet Clinic.

The lady gets out of the car and takes the cat carrier out of the trunk.

Once we enter, the door makes the sound of ringing bells. I go to the corner of the carrier to hide. Then the moving all stops at once.

"Mittens, the veterinarian would like to see you," the receptionist lady shouts.

Mittens flinches. I pet his leg for comfort. The lady picks up the carrier and walks with the person who called up Mittens. Mittens is trembling with fear. We go through a series of halls and end with an unmistakable halt.

The crate for Mittens is set down on a soft mattress. We scramble in an attempt to hide. We scrunch up in the corner of the crate.

Mittens comes out, brushing his tail across my face as

if he is saying good bye. They give Mittens a checkup, and the veterinarian and the lady start to talk in private.

Willie, Ally and I huddle up. What if Mittens is sick? What if he is moribund? That would be the worst thing that could happen to us. I wonder if Willie and Ally think the same. The talking finally stops, and there is an unbearable silence.

I go over and clutch Willie. He is shaking. Ally is tremulous, too. I can tell by her wobbling wings. I look through a tiny hole in the crate and hear the lady and the vet whispering.

"He has to take it. There's no other option," the vet says with a pang of pain in her voice.

"But, why?" the lady questions. "Cause he is quite sick?"

I draw a breath and hear a whisper in a very gentle and calm tone. Willy and Ally do the same. Then I hear a couple of words come out of the vet's mouth.

"Mittens is h-m-m…" That's the words I hear.

I cannot make out what they are saying. I go over to the other corner as Mittens enters the crate.

I realize now is the best time to escape from the dreary plastic container and go find Alvin. I tell them that this is our final chance. They say yes.

We get out of the tiny crate and run onto the hard, stiff, hot ground. It is covered in some weird sticky slop.

Behind-the-Scenes

(Magic Potions and Drinks by the Cobra)

4. The Winty Potion

Have your twin with you in your house with the Winty Potion!

chapter fifteen

FINDING ALVIN

We trudge out of the vile mixture and head over to a bus stop. Maybe we can find a way here. I cling onto a man's coat and we board the bus.

We get off on a street that is called "Stable Way" in hopes that Alvin would come here. Ally, Willie and I go through a hill surrounded by big houses, where big monsters try to hit us fast or blast a bad gust of smoke onto our faces.

Ally flies into the sky and reports that she sees the

stables. Also she sees a path, but there is only one small problem.

It is a long journey across an endless river. I gasp, sputter, and try hard not to burst into tearful, sadistic sobs. The world is gone and I am gone. A gecko and a mouse cannot swim.

But soon I realize that a bird is different. Oh! A bird can easily fly onto the sky and be safe from the danger of the ocean that can drown everything. For a moment, I shiver at the horrifying thought that the ocean can pull Willie and me by the tail right into it. I go up to Willie. His tears make it hard for him to see.

Ally comes over and says, "Come on guys, don't be chicken."

She says with a slightly mocking tone. Willie and I feel hurt. Ally appears to be angry.

"Well, if you're too scared to go, I'm going by myself," Ally says with gusts of emotion coming down her face.

"Are we going?" I ask.

"No," Willie responds, kicking a stone hurtfully on the way.

They both are gone, and I go over to a large area filled with big rocks. I go underground into the dirt where I find a stick. I wedge it between the two edges of the hole.

Within minutes, I start to rest and fall asleep.

I walk north and then west. With no map or compass, I am truly worthless. I sit down and lean against a tree to think. The sky above me seems endless and unbeatable. Sagging my shoulders, I start to sob agonizingly. I don't stop until I hear a lot of stomping and a loud voice sounding like a big carnivore's. I hide in a big bush.

Another voice comes, "But what do we do?" It says with a big stomping noise I have ever heard. I don't dare to make a sound.

"Why did I ever agree to go on this adventure?" I yell in exasperation.

Just then, a humongous dark hairy man comes out from the trees. Actually it is more like a big hairy animal. I wince. The worst part is that he is being followed by another one of those creepy creatures.

I go over to a big hollow tree with a gigantic hole in it. I crawl inside and wait. I can hear the creatures stomp with their big hairy feet right across the trees.

I get a good spot to watch inside the big hollow. I sit right up in a corner and move to the middle of the hollow. I look up and see through a big opening. I wonder what is happening.

Curiosity takes over the best of me, and I climb up the

inside of this big hollow tree with no idea of where I am going or where I will land.

I scream, but it is useless. I look down sadly and see a lake before me. I mean a real lake. In the blink of an eye, I am under the surface of the great lake. I tread water with my arms and feet, vigorously pushing and swirling the water. I go on my back and try back stroke. I would drown if it were not for Ally, who saves me.

Willie is on a little raft with something around his neck. It beeps every five seconds. Then the name hits me. The strange thing is called "a tracker." I go up into the air, clipped between Ally's sharp silver talons, Ally drops me down on the raft.

"Where did you get this?" I ask as I feel the soft orange rubber that can float.

We use the tiny paddles and start to row us back to the shore. By the time we are back, the sun has already gone down. I eat some sweet and tangy berries Willie has served for us. We can suck the juice out of them. I just eat the whole thing including seeds.

"We need to find Alvin," I say urgently to Willie.

Suddenly, the raft tips over. I am once again covered in deep water from head to toe. Who is going to save me now? I actually feel the freezing water. The temperature has just dropped below zero. I think of how hopeless I am, with the water clogging up my nose.

I cannot swim, but I can blow bubbles. I push myself in and blow all the water out. I come out and take one whole deep breath and go back in. I repeat these steps many times until I feel too tired to move.

It's the end of hope. I say to myself.

Just then I see a big boat. It has a deck and some people on it. I look closely at the boat, and I see a window and a little cabin. I also see a little desk with maps on it and a compass. The boat starts to come towards us.

At first sight, I think they are about to rescue us, but I recall my past experiences. Many times I learned that I should never keep my hopes up.

A handsome man looks at us. He is riding a motor boat and his name tag reads "James." The man looks as if he is in his middle ages. He has fine smooth black hair. He comes over and picks us up onto the boat.

He puts me in a vast rainforest in a tank that is just like what I had when I lived at home. Willie is put in something called "a hamster cage" that also looks like the one from home. But I think Ally got the best of us because she is the only one to be able to roam around freely. I am quite jealous.

I hear a very familiar noise. I recognize who it is. Alvin! I go on a branch and jump hard onto the glass wall. My friends whip their heads around and gasp.

"Willie, Alvin's here!" Ally and I yell out.

Alvin puts his hoof in the water when James steers back and places Alvin in a small wooden stable filled with hay.

Behind-the-Scenes

(Magic Potions and Drinks by the Cobra)

5. The Poly-Thorn Potion

Pour this potion into a plant pot and watch your plant grow. To make this potion, mix two packets of plant food with water and shake.

chapter sixteen

GOING HOME

Speechless and aghast, I sit down on the hard floor, and big watery tears are spilling all over my face. If I were a human, I would be on my knees, begging earnestly for a handkerchief. Ally looks amazed. Willie looks white, as white as Swiss cheese. I just sit there, with my mouth open.

My fist shoves into the open air. It bangs against the container, but I really don't care. The gesture seems to send an electrical current through my friends' hearts. My friends cheer, shout, and shove to see a small glimpse of

Alvin drinking water in the stable.

Then things turn even better. When the boat is close to the shore, a tall lady comes over and frees us. I hop up and down in excitement, landing on the beach. We all run to the nearby woods.

I smell something like rotten eggs, so I need to turn away. Dead crickets smell better than this. I only eat live crickets. I am quite picky about my choice of meals, drinks, and scents. My eyes burn and my head feels like it is stuffed with dead crickets and dried-up mealworms.

The smell stops fuming the air. I shake my hand in front of my face to clear up the smell that has stuck to my nose. After I clear up the odor, I see the most terrible thing in the world—the cobra.

I am horrified. Luckily, he doesn't seem to notice my friends and me. I duck behind a polished pot and find that I am okay, but my friends are gone.

Again, hope has disappeared. I feel as if my heart had been pierced with a needle. Not one small speck of hope is left now. I feel truly awful, but I take a tiny peek to see if the coast is clear.

I scamper towards the place where Willie, Alvin, and Ally were standing before they were attacked. I wait a few hours until midnight. At 3:00 a.m., I wish on the brightest, prettiest, fastest shooting star I have ever seen.

The prick of a pin against my finger is like a little burst of pain that will send me flying to the depths of my brain.

A light turns on and clicks off. I close my eyes and yell out my sighs. Then I make a wish for the safety of my friends, the death of the evil cobra, and a healthy amount of food for all of us.

I make a bed out of fresh leaves. After I am satisfied with my work, I take sticks, big leaves, and mud to form a tent. I lie down and take the most comfortable rest in my entire life.

The next day, a letter in a small envelope falls on my tent. I open it, and it reads:

To find your friends, you must look up,
scan the whole sky, and say YUP.
Look for a man covered in moose hide.

Then you must walk past a funny little woman
who says you won't last.
Pay no attention to a girl who is tied to a mast.

Search for a garden that encases a magic golden beet.
You must find a way to crack this treasure,

or nothing you try will make things better.
Ride a bike that speeds up time to the future.

Then, you will find Willie and all your other pals.
You will see a strong man
holding a miraculous silver ball.

Free a lamb from a life-changing curse.
Free her quick, or it might get worse.

I'm not playing a game.
Go to a vast forest with evergreen trees.

You will find a lizard, your own age.
Take her with you.
Don't be afraid.
But whatever you do, don't say her name,
for this is bad luck.

I shiver in fright. I read the bottom of the yellowed and torn letter: "from Poppy, the Moon Girl's messenger."

"Poppy?" I ask myself until my head starts to throb.

I grab my senses and look up. It is early morning. I can tell by how the sun's bright yellow fingers are just touching the clouds.

When I say "Yup," my feet feel light and my eyes feel as if they are about to burst out of their sockets.

Uh, oh! I think I am traveling to another world.

Behind-the-Scenes

(Magic Potions and Drinks by the Cobra)

6. The Selrit Potion

This potion can act like an idea maker. It scribbles down your thoughts and gives you all ideas!

Behind-the-Scenes

(Magic Potions and Drinks by the Cobra)

7. The J.O.P.

J.O.P. stands for Juice of Potion. It is really tasty and can make someone happy!

chapter seventeen

WHO'S THERE?

I close my eyes, and the world before me turns into a big blue blur. I can feel my feet lifting up from the ground. I try my best not to scream or make any reaction to the swirling and dizziness that is set up for me to fall into. The best I can do is not to faint when I leave the real world behind.

"Ouch!" I blurt out when I hit the ground that is covered in a thick layer of sharp grass. I get up and look for the man in moose hide.

I walk towards a big cave that has a big bright-yellow

light coming out of it. I go inside and draw a gigantic breath of the fresh moist stone.

I see a fire to my right and a man with a moose sweater warming his hands by the fire. His skin is the color of dark brown cocoa. His eyes are the color of stars speckled with green.

I make a little noise, and something happens.

The man asks in a deep voice, "Who's there?"

I think it is best not to answer. The hairy and smelly man picks up a large stone and sends it flying right towards me.

Grabbing on to my senses, I quickly dodge the rock. It lands safely four feet behind me, but there are still much more to come. I continuously have to dodge the rocks until I get an idea, not just a plain old idea but a juicy-fresh idea filled with adventure and fun.

I climb up a little mound of stones and hollow it out so I can snuggle in it until the man stops throwing rocks at me.

I stick my tail out of the little fort and yell, "Hello, Mr. Whoever You Are!"

After I say it, with my tail swinging back and forth in a teasing motion, the earth starts vibrating. I can hear the bird's swirling in a vortex above me. My plan has worked.

I make sure my tail is safely secured in a tight crevice and wait for the man to start throwing more rocks. The moment a rock penetrates through my fort, I quickly run out of the cave, leaving the man wondering where I am.

I bump into a tree and find a big bright circle. I struggle to cover my eyes from the blinding-yellow light. In the blink of an eye, everything clears up.

In the place of the bright circle, there is now a lady, the size of a pin. She is wearing a tattered-up shawl and a holey wool hat. She looks wrinklier than an elephant. She is really creepy because she walks around like a zombie and keeps on saying, "You won't last! You won't last!"

I fall into a big hole and find a mini plate with crickets on it. Has somebody been expecting me? I gobble up the crickets, and slowly but surely I start to shrink. I start falling down again into a deeper hole.

I cover my head and try to avoid hitting the falling pebbles pelting down on me. A big rock plummets down from the sky and whizzes by my head. It lands on the floor with a clunk and makes a big hole below it.

I land on the soft dirt and look up. It's pretty dark. I decide to settle here and find a way out tomorrow. I push some dirt to the side and make a border for a rounded bed. I have no snack for tonight.

For some reason, I smell more meaty crickets and some mango. I leap up again and I feel as if something had been lifted off my shoulders. The smell of the crickets and the pleasant chirp of them feels comforting.

I almost feel as if I were back home to my cozy little rainforest. In that place, some crickets are dangerous and some others are pleasant just like the way things should be in our lives. Thinking that I must be dreaming, I close my eyes and take a rest.

Behind-the-Scenes

(Magic Potions and Drinks by the Cobra)

8. Making the Juice of Potion

Combine a can of Sprite with one tablespoon of lemonade mix. Add any flavor of concentrate juice. Mix well and serve cold.

chapter eighteen

WHERE ARE YOU?

I get up and decide to get a meal. I walk around, looking under pebbles and finding small beetles that don't look so yummy.

Now I see a girl—a little girl who is huddling by a poorly lit fire. Her hands are tied up to a large metal pole. Her eyes are hollow and grey. They seem to give off a cloud of gloominess that lingers in the air. Her shirt is faded and ragged. She is wearing a sun hat made out of dirty straw, and her pants are a stormy black. Her whole body takes on a sense of pain and agony.

I clench my hands into balls and run, trying to get that horrid image of the girl out of my mind. I trip on a root in an immense garden plot. The carrots have been mushed. The radishes are rotten. The only thing that has survived is a beautiful, magical beet. Its skin takes on a golden shine, and its texture is smooth to the touch. It looks so much like a star.

I remember the line in the letter: *"Find a way to crack this treasure, or nothing you try will make things better."*

I try everything. I whack it on the ground, kick it, and sit on it. But it does nothing but roll away. I climb a tree and drop the beet from the highest branch. When the beet falls to the ground, it cracks revealing a secret portal. As soon as I jump in, I'm encased in a trap of light.

I gasp, "This is no portal. This is a trick!"

I see a horrible thing—the cobra! I take three big breaths and try to relax. I get an idea.

"Oh, cobra!" I yell out.

I get a hiss in return, and he comes over. I go over to him, but I stick my head accidently in his way. I brace myself for the pain that is to come.

Suddenly, the cobra goes limp. I notice that he is dead. I go over and try to find the heart, but I can't find it anywhere. This can only mean one thing: Willie, Ally,

Alvin, the cobra, and I all do not know where the heart is.

Cautiously, I peer into the golden sky now fading into the dark, miserable distance. I climb out of the light trap and make my way out of the beet to land on the ground.

I am familiar with this ground! Then I realize that this is not ground. It is water. It is blue, shimmery, and overall scary. I start to drown. When I finally get to the surface, I hear something. It is the soft, delicate hum of a wheel moving rapidly. Could this be the bike that speeds up the future?

At the last minute, I jump on. I grab a moving chain that is attached to a whole big bunch of gears and wheels. I fly over to the handle bars and flop onto the seat.

Something magical is happening. The bike is moving all on its own. I am flying towards a rainbow, a beautiful rainbow. I see all the beautiful colors and the swirls of red, orange, yellow, green, blue, and purple.

I see a big spiral of colors. It is wonderful. I get to touch the amazing rainbow as I pass by. It feels like cotton candy.

Cotton candy is fluffy, sweet, and chewy, but only humans are supposed to eat it. Once my friend Tracy, a dog, ate some cotton candy that had fallen on the ground and became very sick. My other friend told me that Tracy had puked all over her owner's shoes. It is the most dreadful thing to me. Tracy went to the vet and recovered in two days.

I take a little rest again. When I wake up, I hear a piercing scream, and the only one who is capable of that scream would be my best friend, Willie.

Behind-the-Scenes

(Magic Potions and Drinks by the Cobra)

9. The Cobra's Soda Drink

This soda is the creepiest but most fun recipe that you will ever make. Making the soda drink started long ago when the cobra's ancestors were thirsty and there was no clean water. We do not have exactly the same ingredients that they used, but we do have recipes!

chapter nineteen

RIDDLES

My friends are screaming, with their mouths open. I catch them and pull them onto the bike. I see a man holding a silver ball and a lamb by its tail.

"To get the lamb and the silver ball, you must solve these riddles. The second one is more like a math problem," the man says.

He hands me a scroll.

It reads: *"I appear once in a year, twice in a week, and zero times in a day."*

The second riddle says:

In a land far away, there are eight hundred fifty witches and ninety five brooms for play. In a world far above, thirty miles away, five trolls are getting their own ways. The trolls grow ten apple trees with five apples every day. Group all the numbers you get by even numbers and odd numbers. For all the even numbers, add them up. For all the odd numbers, subtract each number from the biggest to the least. Then, add up the answers to save your little lamb, Todd.

I look at the piece of paper and see the answer in the word, "year," "week," and "day" for the first riddle.

"It's the letter E!" I blurt out.

"Good," the man says and hands me the silver ball.

Now for the lamb, I reread the question. The numbers are 850, 95, 30, 10, and two 5s. The even numbers are 850, 30, and 10. 850 plus 30 plus 10 equals 890. Then, we subtract 5 from 95 and again subtract 5 from 90. We get 85. Now we add 890 and 85.

"The answer is 975," I yell to the man with a calm, stretched, and clear voice.

"Good job," utters the man.

"Here's the lamb," he says in an irritated voice.

Then something amazing happens. The lamb is turning into a rattle snake. First come the scales, and come the fangs. Finally the rattle snake body. The snake slithers away, leaving a path of sparkling little objects behind.

I stand there speechless. Now the lamb is right beside me again. How could that be? This must explain the curse. I pick up one of the sparkly and shiny objects that the snake has left. I see a question engraved in the center of the object.

It says: *"I am fast and strong. I wreck the rocks in my grasp. All animals depend on me, but alas, I am fierce"*

I think, "What could this mean?"

I look at the sky and everything around me. I see some blue, brown, green, and the faintest bit of yellow. Then I remember blue. Water is blue. The animals depend on water, and rivers can erode stones.

"The answer is a river," I shout to my friends.

They nod in agreement. Suddenly, a piece of the ground opens up and stretches to a far tree. It opens up in segments and gets thinner and thinner. It pops and five more appear. They all stick together and form a maze with several openings. The sparkly cubes are scattered here and there among the rows.

The lamb nuzzles me and leads me to a row with a

sparkly cube in it. I lift it and look under.

It says: *"I have a million spots. I am the color of sand. I am not an animal because I do not live on land."*

I groan, "These questions are getting tougher and tougher each time!"

Willie thinks for a minute.

"I know. The answer is a sponge!" Willie yells.

The lamb leads us through a couple of more paths, and we find the next sparkly riddle cube.

It says:

> *I once had a party. I invited 8 guests and set out some pie plates so much prettier than the rest. I had 78 slices of pie for the guests, my mother, my father, my brother, my sister, and myself. How many slices would each person get? And how many pies would I have if each pie had 3 slices?*

Ally goes over it in her head. At school, she used to be pretty good at this kind of thing. She thinks about what the question is asking. There are 8 guests and 5 members of the family who want the pie. 8 plus 5 equals 13. So, there is a total of 13 people who want the pie. If the man had 78 slices, and there were 3 slices per pie, which means 78 divided by 3 equals 26 pies.

If we want to know how many slices each person

would get, we would have to divide the total number of slices by the total number of people, so we get 78 divided by 13 equals 6.

"The number of pies the man had is 28, and each guest could eat 6 slices," Ally answers with a loud voice.

At that moment, I hear a loud boom, and we are thrown into a vast forest filled with edible greens.

Behind-the-Scenes

(Magic Potions and Drinks by the Cobra)

10. The Cobra's Soda-Drink Recipe

Original ingredients: five eyeballs (can be substituted with peeled grapes), deer beer (Sprite), blood (Kool-Aid drink mix)

Mix all the ingredients and put the grapes into the mixture.

chapter twenty

A MIRROR IMAGE

It is all dark. Willie finds an oil lamp and lights it with some matches. We find some light. Alvin sits down and whispers something to Ally. Ally nods and leads us to a cave.

In a moment, a clap of thunder strikes the top of our cave. Then everything is silent. The sound of water dripping from the roof of our cave brings the color back to our cheeks. Well, not to me, because I don't have cheeks. We decide it's time for our break. I doze off, with the rain singing a lullaby.

When the sun peeks its way through the clouds, we get up and yawn escapes my lips. I scan back to when we were still awake.

"There was no gigantic yellow thing here!" Alvin says.

I kick it. The thing unrolls and climbs up a wall. I notice its shape and its features, and I remember she's part of me.

It was long ago. Probably eight years ago, it happened. But I will never forget it. The most horrible thing happened on that day. While my younger sister Makala was just coming out of her egg, a fierce bird swooped down and picked up the egg with its talons, dropping Makala on the ground. Makala ran away and hid. Seeing what had happened, I hid in a hollow log. The eagle trapped my mother, my father, and my other siblings. I tried to nibble on a pine cone, but it only hurt my mouth. By then, the tears had already started drop by drop. I practically flooded the entire log.

That was the time when my owner family found me. I was ten months old. I was put in a tank and placed on top of the dresser, gingerly cared for and well fed.

Six years later, I set out on the great adventure to try to find the blue tin heart. Now I have met many friends, a danger to Makala.

I bite my lip and answer to Alvin, "Maybe it's just a weird flower. You never know."

Alvin shrugs and adds, "I guess so."

Ally frowns. Willie scampers in circles. When all my friends have their backs turned, I jump onto the wall and quickly cover up Makala with my body.

Just then I start to slip. My head gets in the way. Makala is a lot bigger than I thought. She goes a little forward and accidently licks my chin.

"Eww!"

Ally turns around, her beak flies open in shock.

"What is underneath you?" Ally asks.

"Nothing," I say coldly.

"Somebody woke up on the wrong side of the bed," Alvin says, his tail swinging from side to side.

Willie turns around and mumbles, "I'm hung… What happened to you?"

"Nothing. Nothing at all," I respond, my tail whipping the air.

Ally flies over and pokes me in the back with her talons.

"Ouch!" I exclaim, dropping to the ground, revealing Makala.

"Who is this?" Alvin asks.

"Do you know this creature?" Willie asks, scurrying over.

Makala climbs up higher and dangles her tail above us. Ally pecks at it with her beak. Makala thrashes her tail into Ally's face.

Ally swoops down, puts her face close to mine, and hisses, "This is the meanest animal ever."

I push her away and sit in the corner of the cave, watching the chaos before me. Alvin gets smacked in the neck. I've had my fill of it.

"Stop it!" I scream.

The sound echoes through the walls of the cave, and I can hear the birds flying away. Everything becomes silent.

The minute I open my mouth to explain things, Ally says loudly, "This is all the stranger's fault. If she hadn't whacked me in the face, I wouldn't have hit her."

"Yes," Alvin and Willie both say in agreement.

"No, no, no, no!" I say even louder than the last time.

Ally, Alvin, and Willie stare at me as if I had just grown big fuzzy eye brows and a smooth oiled mustache.

"What?" they all question.

"Do you know this fellow?" Willie asks.

I sigh, I frown, and then I admit it, "This is my sister Makala."

Everybody gasps.

"Why didn't you tell us?" Alvin asks.

"Is that true?" Willie wonders.

"Seriously?" Ally asks.

"She looks just like you," Alvin comments. "You are one mean gecko."

When we turn around, Alvin runs off, brushing past Makala as she falls on his back.

Behind-the-Scenes

(Magic Potions and Drinks by the Cobra)

11. The Cobra Delight

This drink is a pleasant cocktail that is a great healing drink for tail aches and stomach aches.

chapter twenty-one

THE DREADFUL HORSE HUNT

Ally stretches her arms, frowns, and asks me, "Max, do you know where Alvin is?"

I say "no" and go over to Willie.

"Willie, do you know where Alvin is?" I ask him.

"Do I look like I know?" Willie grumbles.

"The only way Alvin could be missing like this is if he got upset and ran away." Ally says.

"So, the real question is who made him upset," I add, trying to hide my guilt.

"First, instead of blaming each other for making Alvin

run away, we should just find him and ask him why he ran away. Then everything will be peaceful." Willie says.

Ally frowns. "Where's Makala?"

At that moment, I hear a vibration in my ear and I know things will not be good. Ally and Willie are hiding behind what looks like a rock but suddenly starts to move.

"Watch out!" I yell to them.

They soon realize what is happening to them and are now coming towards me. I slide my hand far enough to reach Willie's little claws, and we hide in the corner of the cave with no way to go.

I clearly see the rock standing up and revealing a hideous creature. This strange animal has a horn on his head and right on the dead center of his flat-dish-like face. His eyes are as big as teacups and are the color of coal. His body smooths down into a curve and goes back up again into a sort of a swirl. His foul, stinky feet look like big bricks and are as heavy as two steel balls. His teeth made out of pure iron flash, and his stretched-out white lips beam.

I gasp. This reminds me of a story we all had shared in my family for generations until the accident happened with my family.

The story goes like this:

Once upon a time, there lived a wise old man. He had a daughter and an older son. One day, his son went exploring in the woods by their house. When he got to the forest, he took out his axe and chopped up some wood from the finest trees. When he found a good spot for break, he met a girl who had horns and all different ugly features. The boy loved her nonetheless.

One thing the boy did not know was that the girl who he loved was the descendant of Halümtros, the evil sorcerer, and Lydia, the evil queen. The girl's name was Hailey, a pretty name for such an ugly creature. Hailey secretly hated the daughter of the old man, the brother's sister.

One day, she came to the old man's house, and when the old man opened the door, she quickly turned him into a hideous monster by saying these magic words. The magic words could also make the man do whatever Hailey commanded:

Eye of a newt and the tail of a lizard.
An old tree branch and a sizzle of a frizzle.
Take some steel and take some linoleum,
Take the droplets of pandemonium,

And turn this man to one of the monster clan.

The man turned into a monster, and some say he is still alive to this day. Hailey told the monster to go eat his daughter and to leave and never come back. The monster obeyed.

Soon when the brother came home from chopping wood, he found his father eating his sister. "Father, why are you doing this, dear father?"

Hailey cackled just as a thunderbolt struck the house. Then, without a word, she sunk her fangs into the son's leg.

I bolt and I yell for Willie to come right behind me. I am pretty sure that we are ahead of the monster, but I run more just in case. I turn around and see the monster gaining on me. I run faster and jump into a ditch.

I pull Ally and Willie in quickly before the monster comes. I walk around in the ditch and take a peek. The monster is gone. I pull myself out of the ditch and onto the ground. Ally and Willie follow.

Ally, Willie, and I now must start making plans to find Alvin, and maybe Makala. We decide to build a fort so we can talk about things in the warmth. Ally will get big leaves, I will get mud, and Willie will get sticks.

When we all come back with our supplies, I get to work on the fort. I plunge four sticks into the ground and secure them with mud. I use a ripped-up leaf and some mud to apply to other sticks to make the roof. When I am done, I glue the big roof to the four foundation sticks with mud and let them all dry. Lastly, we glue the big leaves to the sides of the fort.

When the fort dries, we lift up the front leaf flap and go inside. We huddle up and Willie gets a fire going inside the fort. I go to sleep, with the red-and-yellow flames breathing out their hot breath on my cheek.

I wake up in the morning to find Ally looking over my head at the land before us. The ground in front of me is cold. There is no warm fire but just black blocks of wood and powdered ash.

"We are in trouble," Ally mutters. I look down past the blocks of wood and black powder. There is a trail of smoke leading to a violently lit-up black-and-red tree. Behind the tree, there lies a single new sapling. Its leaves are now black and crisp. The single tippy top branch is like a candle burning on top from all the way up in our little fort. The smoke coming from the top of the tree billows and curls into shapes of darkness.

We see a little dot appear in the distance. It looks as if

the smoke were trying to swallow the little dot whole. The little dot jumps back and forth as if it is trying to avoid something dangerous. Smoke covers the dot and there are screams of pain ringing in my ears. The little dot comes closer and closer until it reaches the foot of the hill. The little dot comes up the hill slowly, very slowly, and I see the dot is Alvin.

"Alvin!" Ally and I both shout. Willie cheers and screams in delight.

Behind-the-Scenes

(Magic Potions and Drinks by the Cobra)

12. The Cobra-Skin Shake

Have a sip of the past with this shake. Mixed with quality skins from famous cobras, you will make a fortune in your belly with this cool drink.

Behind-the-Scenes

(Magic Potions and Drinks by the Cobra)

13. The Bug-Killing Potion

This potion can kill a whole colony of bugs. It is made from the juice of dead bugs.

chapter twenty-two

THE ONE AND ONLY ZIPPY

Alvin joins us in our fort, and we all listen to Alvin telling us how the problem all started and how he escaped. He ran away from us because he was mad that I had kept Makala a secret in the beginning. But when he turned back, a monster attacked him. The monster took him back to the cave where we stayed and forced him to stay outside.

Alvin heard our screaming and saw us running out. He followed us, but the monster chased him. He had to flee all the way to the field. Out in the field, he saw our fort, but the monster tumbled over him and tried to bite him. He finally kicked the monster in the face with all his might and ran towards our fort. In the distance, he saw the monster dissolve into dust.

At night, I finally build up the courage to ask what happened to Makala. Alvin says she ran and will never come back again.

"Oh…," I say.

I cry in my mind. I try to forget about Makala. It will just be too hard to try to bear a loss when we have an important mission to fulfill. It's hard to forget about the one I was attached to as a sibling.

We all go to sleep. The moment the sun peeks through the big puffy clouds, I wake up and look at the trees. I find a flying gecko and follow it.

I remember a story that was a famous one all throughout the land. It has to do with a flying gecko.

Long, long ago, there lived two very sage geckos. They were a couple, an inseparable gem and an everlasting pair. One stormy night, a merchant gecko moved into the village. He was a very grouchy and heartless man, but he was rich and wore the finest clothes. He, being very rude, absolutely hated the clever pair.

Pretty soon, a rumor was spread throughout the town that the old couple had stolen gold from the mines. The town was shocked. Of course, the rumor was fake. All the geckos who loved the old couple most turned on the couple, all except one caring and kind friend named Zippy.

Zippy was a shape shifter but spent most of his day being a flying gecko. One day, Zippy saw the rich gecko turning in the old couple to the authorities. Zippy flew past the shop owners and other geckos in the town until he got to the rich gecko.

Zippy blew a horn in the rich gecko's ear lobe and the rich gecko fell into a deep sleep. From then on, Zippy was known as Zippy the Flyer, and everybody lived happily ever after.

I now notice something. There's no flying gecko anymore. I'm lost. I'm now truly lost. Frightened, I scamper to a tree and fall into a deep sleep. When I awake, it is daytime. I can't see my friends or anybody I know. I sigh. I go down the tree and pick some berries for breakfast.

I set off to find my friends. This is going to be hard. I can just feel it in my shivering cold bones. It is now raining. I quickly race to make a shelter.

Wait a minute! I smell crickets. I follow the smell to a whole group of fresh live crickets, all for me to enjoy. I eat them quickly one by one, ripping them up in my mouth. It is delicious. I love it.

I go back and start to make a shelter. I look around, trying to find some wood. I cannot find any. I hope there is some wood nearby, or I will be in big trouble.

After I search and look under a bunch of rocks, it turns out that there is no wood here. The rain feels like numbing needles on my skin. I search for some leaves. I pick them up, take the stems, and use them as umbrellas.

I run over to a mushroom on the ground and hide under it. The soil under the mushroom is a bit easier to mould than the hard center soil. I get an idea! Using the softer soil, I dig a very shallow hole around the mushroom.

I make myself comfortable behind the mushroom and lie down in the hole. I do not like being underground, but I guess it will do for now. As I cover myself with leaves, I hear something. The faintest sound of a wolf howl rings in my ears.

I tighten the leaves around me and cover the top of the leaves a bit with soil for camouflage. I get to work, covering all around the mushroom with more dirt. I dive back into the place covered with leaves and snuggle back in. As soon as my tail fits in to the small space in the hole, I hear feet, many feet running fast. I hear another wolf howl more clearly this time. I whimper in fright and roll around. The feet sound as if they were about to trample me—hard.

I hear voices now, "We are almost there. Keep up."

I frown. What are these wolves looking for?

A louder voice says, "We are here, Flying-Gecko Creek."

Flying-Gecko Creek? There is such a thing as Flying-Gecko Creek? I hear the wolves pass, and I venture my way out of the mushroom hole. When I get out, I walk over to some water and drink. A wind blows by, and I get covered by dirt and water which results into mud—wet, sticky mud. The wind knocks me over into Alvin's wet hooves.

"What are you guys doing here?" I mutter with relief, eyeing Ally's soaked wings and Willie's drooping ears. "How did you get so wet?"

"How did you get so muddy?" Willie asks me with a laugh.

"We've got to get going," Alvin says with a frown.

"But first, we've got to clean you up," Ally interrupts.

Ally prepares a basket to use as a basin with leaves

and sun-warmed water from the creek. Alvin creates a brush made with tightly sewn straw. Once I get cleaned up, Alvin reveals an important secret.

He tells us, "An old man in a bubble told us that the heart is in some place called Langley in British Columbia."

That is the place where my own home is. That means now we need to return home from this magical land by any means. How can we do that? We build a raft out of leaves and hay. We pack some berries and set off for the nearest beach. We travel by raft. A bubble of excitement is rising up inside of me. There is a single chance that I could be heading home.

Behind-the-Scenes

(Pixie-Magic Inventions)

1. Is it a Cat or a Mouse?

Do you never know which breed an animal is? With the Animal-Breed Blender, you will be chilling having a mecko or gecko/mouse on your porch.

Part 3
HEART RESTS AT HOME

chapter twenty-three
SETTING FOOT ON THE UNKNOWN

We are not moving anywhere. We are in the middle of the ocean. I look down off the edge of the raft to see fish, many fish. There is also a big white rock in the distance. There could be a beach around it. I suddenly get an idea on how to go faster.

I ask Ally for some leftover hay. Ally gives me a few straws of rich-golden hay, and I carefully weave the thick strands of hay into a net. I use a strong, lengthy stick from the dirty water and attach it to the small net. I skim the net along the water and pull it out.

There are tiny fish squirming and struggling to get out of the net, as I just wanted. I take two bags with holes in them and pour the tiny creatures evenly into the bags.

I split the stick in half and attach them to both of the bags. I clip the sticks to the sides of the raft and get to work, making huge strings with handles for the plankton bags.

I attach the strings to the ends of the bags and see if the fish are still there. I make sure we have a full supply of plankton before testing out my new invention.

Alvin and I pull the strings while Ally and Willie look over and make sure things are going the way they are supposed to. We are on a move.

I tell Alvin to swing right and he does. I swing my left. We make a soft, slow turn to the right and parade on, singing and happily eating berries the rest of the way.

* * *

I guess we have been on the water for about a week. When big ripples start to form, I see a huge fin big enough to drown a six-feet-tall person. I see a sharp, pointed head and black killer-eyes. I also see a white belly and sharp razor-teeth. I realize what this is, and it's not good. It's a shark!

I fill the bags with more plankton to attract lots more

fish. Unfortunately, this makes the shark come closer and closer. The shark looks at the fish and eats them all in one single bite, sending one huge wave which thankfully sends us all the way to the beach.

We get out of the raft, release the plankton, and breathe one last whiff of the salty sea-air. We set off to find the blue tin heart. Our hearts filled with joy, we venture off bravely, releasing a new mission every minute. Our new chapter of life has begun.

We walk farther into the wavy trees, our feet sinking into the golden-grainy sand. Our heads are still sweaty and hot. We walk past two people who have their mouths open.

Alvin says, "They look like ducks!"

A woman falls over, bumping into a tree which sends hard brown coconuts onto the sand, making a soft thump for a landing. I take one. It could be useful in the future.

Willie, Alvin, Ally, and I keep on going through the busy traffic of the beach. More people gape at us through their sunglasses and sunhats. It seems the deeper we go in, the more people that we see start staring, gaping, and gasping.

By the time we pass by Sunday's beach traffic, the sun has fallen past the grey clouds. Ignoring the slight patter of the rain, we walk, not daring to make a sound. The light patter has now transformed itself into extremely heavy rain. We trudge through the muddy ground.

A lightning bolt strikes the middle of the ground, making a crack in the earth, splitting up our group. Willie is now hanging on to the edge of the crack and screaming words that are muffled by the whistling wind.

A twelve-feet-tall monster rises up through the crack between us. I never thought I would have a chance to meet him.

Behind-the-Scenes

(Pixie-Magic Inventions)

2. The Pixie-Style Globe

Point out your next vacation on this magic globe. It will teleport you there!

chapter twenty-four

THE BLACK ONE

He is fierce, cruel, and heartless. Almost everyone in the world knows him. His name is like the flag of evil, pure evil. Everybody calls him by the name of Fire Black, but nobody knows his original name given at birth.

For years, he had been missing. People thought he had been killed. But now he is here. In the depths of the earth, he is rising up through the crack of the century, his killer-eyes meeting ours.

Willie is at my side and Alvin on Ally's. The crack in

the ground gets bigger and bigger each time he goes farther up. I blink. Ally stares. This is not going well…

I do the first thing that comes to mind. I bolt and drag Willie along with me. Willie groans. I keep on pulling him along. He is getting slower and heavier with each painful step. I don't know if we are far enough to take a break, but I do anyway. It is just too tiring.

We stop to rest under a dark brown tree with drooping leaves. It's not the best, but it's all we can do for now. I lie down and take a little nap, with Willie snoring on top of me.

When we wake up, it is just the crack of dawn. The sun is peeking through the horizon when Willie and I are on our feet, searching for Ally and Alvin and trying to stay away from Fire Black. Hopefully, our friends have not been attacked by Fire Black yet. But anything can happen, and this can surely be one.

Willie and I walk on the soft dirt. The area is now filled with strange creatures—tall creatures, small creatures, creepy creatures, and whatsoever. The trees are filled with life, especially birds—colorful, magnificent birds. We see other animals like monkeys, bees, butterflies, and many plants such as flowers, coco trees, and plain bushes.

We walk past the beautiful array of nature set before us into a place with more sand and spiky plants than I have ever imagined.

There are lizards, birds, and we feel the hottest atmosphere in the entire world. I think I might die of heat exhaustion.

"It is so hot," Willie complains in a whiny voice.

"I hope Ally and Alvin are here, too." I say.

I am cold-blooded, which means my body temperature changes as to the temperature of the area I am staying in. Willie is warm-blooded, so his body temperature stays the same no matter what. Technically, Willie's body is colder than mine right now because his blood is still boiling hot but not as hot as the desert.

After ten minutes, Willie starts begging me for water. I sigh. I wonder if I can use the coconut I got from the tree. I roll it over in the sand, but nothing happens. I kick it. Still, nothing happens. I punch it. Again, nothing happens. I scratch it against a cactus. Something happens. A little hole is formed in the shell and reveals a sloshy white coconut-drink that looks quite refreshing. I take a sip. I let Willie take one, too. It's delicious.

We walk along, enjoying the new white coconut-milk that we just cracked open from the shell. It is starting to become dark. The sun is disappearing from the sky, leaving a trace of white to rule the stars. We keep going until Willie is too tired to go on.

We take a break, and when we wake up, the setting is much different. There is no sand and my bottom feels numb. The ground is white and fluffy but the sky is dark. Could this be the Artic?

I lift Willie up by the hand and let him see the transformation that has happened. There is a dark sky, and snow is falling down on us in pretty small flakes that are about as thin as dust. We track foot prints in the snow. Our hands are cold and numb and our feet feel sore.

Too sore to move, Willie and I both crawl on the ground, lifting our knees up and moving them back down. We are still going in the distance. I see a small white structure made out of blocks of ice. It is sparkling in the bright sky.

We quickly try to move towards it. When we are about ten feet away from the block structure, the most dreadful thing happens in front of us—Fire Black!

Behind-the-Scenes

(Pixie-Magic Inventions)

3. The Sports Bowl

The sports bowl is now a huge fad in the pixie world. It is a bowl made out of safe material and there are four TV screens in the center. All you have to do is to choose your four favorite sports you want to watch from the buttons at the top of the bowl. They will magically pop up on the screens.

chapter twenty-five

SCARLET

My face is so close to his. I can smell his foul meaty breath, and I am pretty sure Willie is suffering from the breath, too. Fire Black's hand swipes past my face, barely missing it by an inch. Willie's tail is swinging back and forth while he chews his lip in nervousness.

Just when Fire Black is about to crush me with his foot, someone familiar flies in from above. Her hair is fair, and today she is wearing a light blue dress with sparkles on it designed to look like stars.

Moon Girl swoops in, pushes Fire Black away, and hands me an envelope sealed with a star-shaped glittery-yellow sticker. I gingerly pry open the top flap and peek into the pocket. I unfold the letter on the inside. It reads:

Home is a lucky place.
Freedom is allowed, roam where you roam.
But different parts of the world you are in
are not so much special than home.
Courage is first place.
Faith is also precious.
With those you might earn a true gift.
Work hard to reveal it.
Work hard to make things bright.
Anything you do could be wrong or right.
Work things out and use your wisdom.
Look closely.
A clue could be under your bed.
The gift is dwelling
where you would least expect it.
Think hard to keep it.
Think well to receive it.

P.S.: Pull the spring in the envelope.

I pull the tiny silver spring inside the envelope. The spring magically disappears and is replaced by a small box. I throw away the envelope and open the red box. Inside, there is a miniature glass bottle with a cork in it.

I look closely inside the bottle and see a tiny pixie. Her wings are gauzy, shimmery, and blue. Her hair is a light shade of magenta. Her eyes are dark blue. She is wearing purple eyeshadow, and she has a short pointy nose. She is wearing a short dress with a pretty gauze layer on top touched with sparkles. She has on a light pink sweater and a diamond pendant with a golden chain.

There is a note on top of the cork: *"Here's a little friend to help you."*

Willie stares at the pixie for a long time. He pulls the bottle from me and looks at the pixie in disbelief.

"This can't be happening," he says.

I take it from him and put it in the snow.

"I wonder…Never mind," I mutter.

I shake my head and carry the cork bottle with me all the way to the igloo. The inside of the igloo is warm, welcome, and bright. Strangely, no one is inside. Willie and I make our way inside the igloo. We both lie down and go to sleep.

The moment we wake up, the pixie is shaking the cork

bottle in my hand. Her hands are punching the glass surface, and she is fluttering all about. When I pull out the cork from the bottle, the little pixie flies out. The pixie flies around in circles and yells something that I can't hear in my direction.

"What?" I ask.

"My name is Scarlet," she shrieks.

I rub my ears. That was painful.

"My name is Max," I mutter back.

Scarlet skirts around Willie's head and frowns.

"Where are we?" she demands.

"In an igloo," I absentmindedly reply.

"Oh!" Scarlet exclaims with a twinge of disappointment in her voice.

"I have to tell you something," Scarlet says. "It's a story."

"We don't have time for stories," Willie snaps.

"No, this is urgent," Scarlet begs.

"Fine," Willie says.

Behind-the-Scenes

(Pixie-Magic Inventions)

4. The Genie Bottle

Make up a wish with this bottle, and your wish will come true just like the legend says. If you are too greedy, you'll be in trouble!

chapter twenty-six

THE THREE HEARTS

Scarlet's face turns misty as she tells us the story.

Long ago, life was dark and cruel in the forest. Terror was spread throughout the land, and you couldn't even walk a mile without hearing a single scream. But there were certain types of happiness in life, and birth was one of them.

One day, Marcus Phil—a rich, snobby man with the bushiest mustache you could ever find—walked into his garden to find his roses dead. There was some poisonous sparkling dark purple dust left in trails on one of the petals.

Seeing his roses dead, Marcus was indeed furious. Marcus screamed, bellowed, and shouted. Once he finished screaming, his heart was pounding and his throat was sore. Seconds later, Marcus fell down dead.

The minute Marcus landed on the ground with a thud, a baby bird hatched in a nest nearby. After the cruel man's death, a droplet of pure kindness was born. This little creature's name was Eloise. Eloise was the symbol of kindness. A few moments after giving birth, Eloise's mother flew off to explore and wander around the human world.

Eloise was left alone. She was quite content of what she had. As time passed, Eloise learned by herself how to fly, starting by fluttering off the nest for a few seconds. By the time she was five in bird years, she was a full-fledged flyer.

Once she became old enough, she packed up her belongings and set off to find a new home. Her belongings were magical. But if they were put in the wrong hands, they could be fatal. They were three beautiful tin hearts all in different colors—a red heart, a green heart, and finally a blue heart.

The red heart had the power to make you invisible for a short period of time. The green heart had the power to kill or heal living things on command. And the best one of them all was the blue heart. It had the power to summon anything you want anytime, but it could only be used in emergencies. It could also be used as a passport to enter magical world.

Eloise was now old and frail. For the hearts' sake, she buried them all in a ditch. Over time, layers and layers of earth swished and toppled on top of the hearts, and soon the hearts were fully buried.

Today, although Eloise is not alive, her great-great-granddaughter is still out there somewhere.

As expected, there would be a battle for the three hearts to find and retrieve them, and you are in the battle, too. That is the story of the truth.

Scarlet frowns and sighs.

"That's the only reason why Luna brought me here," she says.

"Luna?" Willie and I both ask at the same time.

"You don't know Luna? Oh, you must know her as Moon Girl!" Scarlet remarks.

"Oh, Moon Girl? We know her," Willie says.

"So, do you now have no purpose here?" I ask.

"Well, I have done my job, but I guess I could stay a while. If you want me to," Scarlet says.

"Can you help us with something?" Willie asks.

"What?" Scarlet asks.

"We kind of lost our friends, Ally and Alvin," I say guiltily.

"Oh, I can totally help with that!" Scarlet exclaims.

"Hang on, it's in here somewhere," Scarlet responds, digging her hand into her pink sweater.

"Whoa!" Willie mutters under his breath.

Scarlet giggles, "Everyone says that."

After she pulls out a sparkling jewel pixie-phone, she hisses into the screen, "Ultra Navigator 5000, three o'clock, into pink sweater pocket."

A few seconds after Scarlet flies down onto a log, she pulls a huge camera-like thing out of her sweater. It is a light green color and has many gadgets attached to it such as the satellite dish on the top left corner, the control button, the portable speaker, the camera screen, the bug net, the doughnut ring, the stand, and finally the magic pixie-dust stored in the bottom for emergencies.

Scarlet pushes some buttons on the screen and types in a couple of codes.

"How do you spell your friends' names?" Scarlet asks.

"Simple," I say. "A-l-l-y and A-l-v-i-n."

Scarlet types the names in, her tiny fingers flying over the teal–colored keyboard.

"Done," she says.

She puts her eye in the camera lens and whispers something into the portable speaker. A minute later, she sprinkles some pixie dust on top of our heads and pulls out a clear-silver ice wand from her pink sweater.

She waves the wand and yells, "Dinifem!"

Thin white-and-blue sparks start bursting out of Scarlet's wand and form into a thick, pulling tornado.

Behind-the-Scenes

(Pixie-Magic Inventions)

5. Backpack Ultimate

This backpack is definitely for winners. With its ability to come to your hand from a distance, getting to pixie school and learning spells would be a breeze. To make this, hot-glue magnets to your backpack and gloves.

chapter twenty-seven

THE PRESENT AND THE PAST

I land on the ground with a thud. The swirling silver tornado is now floating upwards into the sky. I wait for my eyes to focus and see a smooth landscape with many trees.

I feel a sudden breeze that is ruffling the grass on the ground. I hear hooves when four of them come towards me. I hear the constant flapping of a bird's wings next to the steady beat of the hooves. They are both coming towards us.

I soon notice that the hooves belong to Alvin, and the

wings belong to Ally. I sit down bewildered by my surroundings. Alvin grins. Ally sits down beside me and covers my eyes with leaves. I immediately fall asleep, but this time I have a dream.

I am resting on a tree branch when something with big green eyes swoops down and nips my feet. I jump from the tree and run. I run faster and faster until I see something. At first I think it is a cloud, but as I get closer, I make out a holographic image of a girl with a blurry, tearful expression on her milky-white face.

"Why? How?" the girl asks me.

I stare at her. She stares back. Then the creature that tried to attack me swoops up and down over the image of the girl until all I can see is black. That's when a ghostly little bird appears. It reveals the image of the girl. She is now holding a scroll with a poem on it. It reads:

Animals, poachers, things of all kinds,
rivaling every day.
Poachers respected, animals killed,
poachers paid, animals sold.
We must put a stop to
this gruesome war, the sadness, the fury

that happened once more.
A poor little bird flying here one day.
I told her to leave.
I warned her not to stay.
And today,
I grieve the death of poor little Robin May.

Finally, the poem vanishes, and so does the girl.

I wake up as soon as something hard hits me on the back of my head. I pick it up and look at it. It is a stone which letters and symbols engraved on.

I trace the letters with my finger and recite them out loud: "EGCKO XMA, GRENEVE SI NI"

"What kind of stone would say that?" Ally asks.

"Maybe it's in code," Willie replies.

"I wonder who put it on there," Scarlet says, scratching her chin.

"Whoever did, they are trying to tell you something," Alvin says.

"Well, I'm really glad we could all find each other, but I'm sleepy. Good night!" Ally yawns, rubbing her eyes.

Slowly but surely Alvin and Willie start to fall asleep. Scarlet and I are the only ones awake.

"What do you think those letters mean?" I ask her.

"I don't know, but maybe this machine will," Scarlet whispers as she pulls out her wand and a huge device.

It looks like a crank attached to a screen.

Scarlet takes her wand, waves it, and asks me, "What were those letters, again?"

"EGCKO XMA, GRENEVE SI NI," I answer.

Scarlet flips her wand over and uses the pen-like diamond stud at the bottom to write the letters in. This is the result:

EGCKO XMA, GRENEVE SI NI.

Scarlet swipes at the screen, and this happens:

GECKO MAX, REVENGE IS IN.

Scarlet gasps, "Something bad will happen."

Behind-the-Scenes

(Pixie-Magic Inventions)

6. Swords 8000

These swords can slice through steel and are bewitched to come back to the owner's hand when commanded.

chapter twenty-eight

EVELYN PEARL

My eyes feel heavy when Ally tells me it's time to go.

"Where are we going, anyway?" I ask, shielding my eyes from the bright sun with leaves as I stand up.

"To a shelter. We can't just sleep in the wilderness again. We need to find a shelter," Ally snaps.

"Okay," I say.

"I'm hungry," Willie moans.

"We could stop for breakfast," Ally suggests, her

stomach rumbling in agreement.

We stop at a tree stump and use it as a table. Ally and I go off to pick berries while Willie and Alvin start cleaning off the tree stump and making seats by carving out fallen wood. When Ally and I come back, our hands are full with juicy, aromatic blackberries.

Willie and Alvin have set thick leaves for plates, and on the plates are five roasted nuts each. Willie and Alvin have also collected dead worms for Ally, dead crickets for me, hay for Alvin, and small mushy apples for Willie. All the foods are being roasted over a small fire.

We eat our food in silence. I can hear Willie nibbling constantly on one of his soft apples, and Ally is very loudly slurping her worms as if they were spaghetti noodles. After I finish eating, my full stomach induces me to fall asleep, and again I have a dream.

I'm floating in midair above the ocean. I see fish trapped in nets and people gazing at something below the dark, gleaming surface of the water. I see many boats enough to fill five houses.

On one of the boats, people are hauling up a dolphin with beautiful blue fins and a greyish-black dorsal fin. I see a problem in the tail. There's a deeply blasted black hole in it.

A little while later, a girl comes out onto the deck. She is screaming, yelling, and kicking at the men who pulled out the dolphin from the ocean. I see the redness in her face—the scarlet burn that is taking over her hands and arms. The lush pink rage is tipping off her ears.

"HOW COULD YOU?" the girl protests.

The whistling wind pierces my ears as I drop slowly into the freezing-cold water. With a splash, I fall in. As I quickly resurface, I hear voices.

"We could have made so much!" a man shouts in a husky voice.

I see another man push the girl off the deck. Soon I hear the girl scream in pain as she falls into the water.

I wake up to find my arms, my legs, and my tail extremely wet.

"It was real," I say, panting.

I roll over onto my back. Ally, Alvin, and Willie are staring at me. Scarlet is sitting down, curled up in the dirt. Her lips are pursed and her fists are clenched.

"Something is here," she hisses at the dirt.

"What?" I say.

I go over to where Scarlet is. Right in the dirt, I find a

glass ball. I pick it up and stroke it. Ally, Alvin, and Willie do the same. A crack breaks through in the ground, and we all fall through, with Scarlet right behind us.

It is dark. We have reached the bottom of this strange pit, and we are now trying to find a source of light. Willie picks up a rock, throws it in the air, and screams. Ally pulls a stick out from the wall and examines it. She rubs the stick hard against the wall. Bit by bit, a small light is forced into the thin air. We follow the light and accidently bump into Ally.

"Ow!" Ally whines.

"Be quiet!" I scold.

I stumble on a rock and hear a high-pitched scream. I get up quickly and listen for footsteps. It is all quiet. The moment I put my hand away from my ear, I hear a stampede of feet coming towards my friends and me.

There are a number of voices out in the distance, and one of them sounds very familiar. I think back to my dream when the men pulled the dolphin onto the boat, the girl screamed. I hear that same scream again.

There is the sound of fury and madness in the air. The footsteps have become much louder and vibrant than before. Millions of feet sound as if they were prepared to run, fight, and finally destroy.

I brace myself for the thing or the person that will hit. I wait, but nothing happens. I take a tiny peek out into a room, and there is nothing but one small object—the glass ball.

I gasp, "It is all different."

Ally, Alvin, Willie, and Scarlet follow me as I enter the room with mirrors on the walls adorned with beautiful jewels and gemstones. I see the crystal ball and an elaborate huge mirror in the middle of the room.

There is one thing strange about this room as if somebody painted the room with a brush dipped in some kind of stringy, sticky white liquid and covered the room up with gloominess. Suspicion rises inside me.

I walk towards the crystal ball and see something in it. It is horrifying. It is the girl I saw in my dreams. I look at the girl in the crystal ball.

Then I have a flashback from my dream: *"How could you?"*

A voice pierces the air, and I know its owner. I run quickly, quicker than ever before. I stop abruptly when I see a chamber that has aged skulls, brown skulls, and in the center, a pearly-white skull with an ornate pink bracelet resting on the top.

I hear voices as I fall down asleep. I have another

dream, but this one means something.

I am sitting on a rock with a soft, smooth bird in my hand. The bird is tiny, smaller than a dime. I put the bird down beside me, and the bird flies away. The bird is gone. I walk along a path, my high spirits pulling me up with each little leap. I come to a dead end, and there is the strangest thing in front of me—a waterfall.

It is not just the waterfall that is strange but it is the place inside the waterfall. There is a door, a small round wooden door. I open the door carefully and take a tiny peek at what is in front of me.

There is a chair, a window, and a small fireplace in the room I am standing in. Feeling mist on my skin, I move quickly away from the door. The mist returns. I sit on the chair and look away from the mist. At first, it is small. Then it starts to grow rapidly. The mist waves itself around. It is now in threads.

The threads are braiding themselves together and are now weaving themselves into the words:

EVELYN PEARL, THE GIRL FROM YOUR DREAMS IN LIFE.

My tail flicks up and then rests down. A scream escapes my lips. The threads are still weaving themselves:

TO GET THE HEART AND
TO GO HOME,
FOLLOW ME WHERE I ROAM.
YOU MUST SAVE ME AND
DON'T THROW ME IN THE AIR.
THE RESULTS WILL BE
WORSE THAN A NIGHTMARE.
PULL THE LEVER OF THIS MACHINE.
THEN YOU WILL FACE WITH ME.

Behind-the-Scenes

(Pixie-Magic Inventions)

7. The Fun Box

This box is a blast to have around whether you want a fan, a ball or even doughnuts. The fun box has them all.

Behind-the-Scenes

(Pixie-Magic Inventions)

8. Making the Fun Box

Fill a box with your favorite objects and cut a hole at the top. Decorate the box with felts and stickers.

chapter twenty-nine

A GLOWING CONNECTION

I wake up as I feel some soft thread between my fingers. There is a spool of string and a card.

The card reads:

FOR YOU, THE STRING FINDER 500

I look down at the thread and look at the back of the card. The card shows a diagram of the String Finder 500 on it. A piece of thread has many different layers such as the white base string, the magical communication thread, and finally the magical detector strings.

"Cool!" I say out loud.

"Are you okay?" Scarlet asks me, fluttering above my head.

"How did you guys get here?" I ask Ally.

"We used some kind of pixie machine," Ally responds.

"It was so much fun going through those pathways with pixie dust," Alvin snorts, the bright gleam of his eyes shining in the sunlight.

"No, it wasn't. That made my stomach hurt so much," Willie mumbles.

"It was okay," Ally says, her arms crossed, looking stern and grouchy.

"How did you notice I had been gone?" I ask, scratching my chin in thought.

"Well, Scarlet was following you and saw you fall. She flew back to us, and we tried to get to you," Willie explains.

"But then we got lost, so Scarlet used the pixie machine for us," Alvin mentions.

"So, now we are right here all together again," Scarlet says, crossing her arms with pride.

The string in my hand starts wiggling furiously. It shimmies out of my hands and starts to glow. At first, it is dim and starts to become brighter and brighter until it lights up the whole room. The pink bracelet shines like a lightbulb, illuminating almost everything.

The light goes out, leaving a path of string on the ground in front of us.

"Let's follow it," I suggest.

Ally gives a curt nod, and they follow me as I slowly attempt to follow the glowing string. We are led into a downward staircase. Finally the string ends into a low but very spaced-out cave. I roll up the string into its spool and look around my surroundings.

I see a huge machine that has a lever, a small glass spare container, and a big red plastic cube with Evelyn's pitiful face in the center. I need to get her out. Willie gingerly touches the red cube, and he is instantly pulled into the container.

"We've got to save him!" Ally cries with determination and strength in her voice.

Ally flies above the container and pokes it with her talons. Moments later, Ally gets sucked into the container.

"I will smash that container with my hooves until they are free!" Alvin thunders, his mane quivering with fury.

Alvin runs towards the container. His hooves make a loud clamor as they crash into the container, causing a jagged crack to appear on the glass. As expected, Alvin, too, gets sucked in.

"What do we do?" I ask Scarlet.

"I'll use my wand," Scarlet utters.

She mutters something under her breath and gives a nervous flick of her wand. Then everything goes black.

"This machine has some kind of magic force field. Try pulling the lever," Scarlet croaks.

"Okay," I say in a tremulous voice, and I see she gets sucked into the container.

Shocked, I trudge over to the lever. My hands are quivering with fear and my lip is wobbling up and down as I timidly touch the lever and immediately pull it back. I take a deep breath and wait for something to happen.

I hear voices, screams, and shouts. Evelyn is out of the red cube and is sprawled out on the ground. The world seems to spin like a top, and my eyes go blank as the world seems to swallow me in one vigorous whirlpool bite. I am now forced into the container.

Behind-the-Scenes

(Pixie-Magic Inventions)

9. The Disk 5000

This disk has all the new pixie jams like "Charmed to Be Yours," "Cursed to the Heart," "Spell Me Now," and many more. Take this to the beach, park, and pixie land to rock your heart out.

chapter thirty

THE WHOLE WIDE WORLD

My foot is already sore minutes after I start screaming.

"Ow, watch it!" I groan as Willie comes, toppling on top of me.

Soon, it is all dark again. I hear more voices and my feet turn numb. We are stuffed into the container, and I press my nose against the glass. My breath turns to fog and the wind is terrifying me.

Snow is whipping itself against the glass, and I am afraid that the hail will start to crack the fragile glass container we are in. As the container starts spinning quickly, the snow, wind, and hail disappear in a blur.

We land with a thump onto a rock, and I wait for the container to crack. However, all that happens is we fall into icy cold water. The water is mingled with green and has the fresh scent of seaweed and seashells.

We start to sink into the depths of the ocean, and the air is slowly moving our tank.

"We're going to die in here!" Alvin shrieks, pounding against the glass.

"Oh, be quiet," Scarlet snaps. "I can fix this."

"Easy for you to say. You've got a magical stick that does wacky things," Willie scowls, kicking a lone rock inside the container.

Scarlet ignores Willie and whispers, "Levandra!"

Cracks appear on the glass, and water starts pouring in. Murky water turns to clear water as it touches the surface of the crystalline glass tank.

"Everybody dip your head into the water," Scarlet sings, obviously happy about something.

My head hits the water as I hear Willie screaming.

"Owww!"

I come out of the water with an enormous bubble on top of my head.

"Now you can all swim without drowning yourselves," Scarlet giggles. "That will teach you not to insult the wand, Willie."

We swim out of the broken tank and keep on swimming. We are moving past a school of angel fish when Willie stops abruptly.

"The undertow," Ally whispers.

"Let's go faster," Alvin says.

"Okay," Scarlet says, "whiky!"

Scarlet waves her wand, and on each of our feet, two rocket shoes appear.

"Just press the button on the left side of the boot, and you'll be flying in no time," Scarlet says, pressing the button on her own.

My finger touches the button, and instantly, I fly into the air. I hover for a few seconds.

Scarlet asks me something I have never expected, "Where do you want to go next?"

"I don't know," I say hesitantly.

But a voice inside me croaks out loudly: "H*ome, I want to go home!"*

"Do you really don't know?" Scarlet asks, looking worried.

I glare at Scarlet and whimper, "I want to go home."

The next moment, a dazzling thing happens.

Scarlet hands us one mushroom umbrella and proudly says, "The toadstool parachute, commonly used for travel in the pixie world. Just hold the handle really tight and say clearly where you want to go."

I pull the handle and yell out, "Home!"

When I lift off, I press the buttons on my rocket boots. With my friends, I blast off into the air, my tail swinging in happiness.

Behind-the-Scenes

(Pixie-Magic Inventions)

10. The Me-Seat

This ultimate recliner can fold into anything with just the touch of a button.

chapter thirty-one

HOME AT LAST

The parachute bobs up and down, and the view below me is spectacular. I see many trees, wild flowers, and animals. From up high, the world looks like a giant mosaic, with little dots of green, blue, pink, and white all mixed together to a beautiful piece of art.

As the parachute lowers, I see familiar people, sand, and water. The dots of people's heads move rapidly, and I see the water lapping up the sweetness and joy of the scene.

I am hanging over a beautiful sunny park filled with children who are either doing the monkey bars or riding down the slide. Their smiles are bright and happy. A couple of other children are blowing the seeds off the dandelions. The seeds fly into the air, are suspended for seconds, and then fall to the ground, almost replaying the enjoyable scene.

The parachute moves on towards a small house. The door opens after the parachute touches the door. Finally I am home! I approach a small but jungle-like tank with green leaves sprouting out from everywhere. There is also a long squiggly branch that leads to a small cave.

The parachute drops me inside, and a few moments later, my friends appear. I walk across the branch and see something in the cave. When I enter the small U-shaped rock structure, I see a small dusty tin heart. It is here, finally!

I smile, Ally beams, and Scarlet laughs. We have done it all together.

"Guys, what is this?" Ally stammers.

Everybody stares at Ally. She is pointing at a little slip of paper.

"It is addressed to you," I tell Ally.

"Really?" Ally asks with surprise.

Ally unfolds the paper and reads in a clear voice:

Dear Ally,

I hope you find my gift amusing. I present to you and your friend Willie the most cherished item I have ever carried on my feathery back. It has wonderful powers that I hope you will use in the most needed times.

I was the ghost who stole the heart back after the cobra took the heart during your flight back home. And then I killed the cobra when Max almost got attacked in the old bar's vegetable garden. All the cobra saw was a big white blur.

I am the original owner of the three hearts. I owned the stunning red heart that has the power to make you invisible for a short period of time. The elegant but dangerous green heart can kill and heal living things on command. And the most cherished heart is the blue heart. Its powers are beyond explanation. It can summon anything beyond reach. It is also a passport to anywhere.

For the hearts' sake, I hid them in a ditch. Layers and layers of wet sand went over the hearts and hardened over time into a cave.

Hundreds of years ago, this blue heart was fortunately retrieved by Willie's great-great-great-grandfather down in the cave.

I still do not know where the other red and green hearts went. But what I know is this blue heart is the most precious one that represents courage, kindness, and friendship. I myself am also linked to the blue heart, a symbol of kindness.

Remember that as long as you have the heart, I am always with you, and peace will stay with the world.

Love,
Your great-great-grandmother, Eloise

"I thought that it was my heart," Willie barks.

"All that matters is that we did it all together. We traveled far and wide and found out the truth, the truth about what had really happened," Alvin tells us.

"Let's go to sleep now. I'm tired," Ally groans.

"Me, too," Scarlet yawns.

I lay my head down on the smooth green leaf I am using as a pillow. As I fall asleep, excitement runs through my blood, through my heart. The world is calm and peaceful. I am at home and everything is perfect.

Night is falling. Scarlet prepares goodies and no-heat fireworks. The fireworks are blasted into the air and look like little balls popping into works of art as soon as they reach the world.

Out the window, the stars are bright and there is not a single cloud in the sky to disrupt the cheerful atmosphere of this moment. People have just walked down from the stairs, and Scarlet immediately turns off the fireworks.

My friends and I are lifted up into safe, warm hands. The aroma of food is in the air, and I remember all the meals my friends and I made. My head bursts with joyful memories as the sky stays bright, and food is stuffed into my open mouth.

Happiness is swallowed down my throat. I grab my friends' hands and I sense that what we did was significant to other generations.

But at this very moment, all that matters is now. All

that matters is us and the ones we love. Any type of quest that we are given will need others who back it up to make it happen.

Even if it took time for us to learn the truth, we have accomplished our mission with pride. During our quest, we also learned how to care for one another in difficult times. We have become true friends and will stay together for eternity.

Behind-the-Scenes

(Pixie-Magic Inventions)

11. The World Clock

This clock can tell the time in Asia, Africa, and Loliland in one wave of your wand.

ACKNOWLEDGEMENTS

Diane Lee, I could not have done this without you. If I had a blue tin heart, I would give it to you, no matter what. Thank you for your constant accommodation of me and your sincere and critical advice in editing my work.

Thanks to James Lee, too, who celebrated so wholeheartedly after I finished writing this book. I did not like taking so many photos, but I did like the reason why you made me do so.

I also would like to thank my own gecko Max, the real star, who made writing this book so fun.

Writing this book did not seem like working well in the beginning, but a timeless adventure to places of my imagination fascinated me to get going. I also loved my own dynamic characters that were created by me but somehow strengthened me in many ways.

Finally, I thank YOU for your support by showing interest in my life's work.

ABOUT THE AUTHOR

Jennifer Lee started her writing career at a very early age. Between her age of three and four, she showed her precocious ability in reading and writing with a good sense of rhythm and elaboration. Her talent in writing was clearly revealed after she started her school as she often presented her own poems and stories at her school events. Year after year, her voluminous daily reading boosted her even more polished writing skill.

Finally in 2015 when she was eight years old, she started to write her first novel, *A Gecko's Dimension,* to publish. Her completion of the book took a year and a half.

She was a grand winner of the 2015 Scholastic Canada Haiku Contest. She also spoke at the 2016 TEDx LangleyED event with the topic, "My Best Friend Max." Jennifer Lee's TEDx speech is closely related with this book since her creation of the story was inspired by her pet gecko Max, mentioned in her speech as well.

She lives in Langley, British Columbia with her parents and her one and only Max.

My Best Friend Max

Jennifer Lee's Speech at 2016 TEDx LangleyED

Good morning, all the participants of TED-X Langley conference. I'm Jennifer Lee, and I'm in the third grade. I represent R.C. Garnett Elementary at this honorable event. I'm truly honored to be speaking here today.

Before I start, I would like to ask you a little question. Do you like animals? If you do, you might like this speech. It is about my pet gecko Max.

Max is a crested gecko. The first day I got my gecko, I named him Max. Before I got Max, I felt nervous. I had never had a pet before. "Would it bite? Would it be scary?" I wondered. My mom recommended a pet fish, but I didn't want a fish.

I begged and begged my mom to get a lizard. At that time, I did a lot of research on how to take care of pet lizards. One of the interesting things I found is that they can live up to five to fifteen years, and most of them are gentle and harmless pets to humans. I thought I can enjoy quite a long time with my lizard. But my mom said it would take a lot of responsibility. I promised that I would take really good care of it.

When I saw all kinds of lizards at the pet store, I said to myself, "I want that one. I want that one. I want that one." I finally spotted one last gecko and said, "Now I definitely want this one." The day we brought him home was the best day ever.

We had already set up Max's terrarium before we brought him, and the next day, I went upstairs and whispered to him, "you are so cute." That night I fell asleep dreaming about Max. Since I got Max, I've really been working hard to take care of him. I help my mom when she cleans his home and feeds him. I also mist his home every day a little in the morning and a lot at night.

I have a gecko named Max. At Christmas, he is holly, and in summer he is jolly. I have a gecko who likes the rain and the sound the raindrops make when they land on your umbrella. I have a gecko who is my best friend.

Also if you are afraid of some kind of animal, try going near it, and you will find a big difference in you. By the way, remember to say "I love animals every day!"

SELECTED POEMS WRITTEN BY JENNIFER LEE

Crunchy Leaves in the Fall

Fall is my favorite season because of
the music crunchy leaves make.
They make beautiful music when they fall.
They make me happy and fill my bucket.
This bucket is invisible but it's a magic bucket.
The crunchy leaves dance under my feet,
filling my shining bucket,
fulfilling my autumn dreams.

(Written at age 5)

Rainbows

Rainbows make a burst of light,
so colorful
with a burst of sight.

Oh! Rainbow, so high!
Won't you come down from
the sky to bless the creatures?

A colt so lively and quick,
prancing with its hoofs and tail.
Flowers bloom with a burst of gifts,
giving the forest animals
a pretty lift.

(Written at age 6)

Having Fun in the Snow

Snow, so light and so fluffy.
Water has turned into ice,
giving a pretty glow.
Snowflakes fall from the sky,
all different in shape and size.
A pretty glistening world
where snow and ice mix together.
A festival happening so fast.

(Written at age 7)

Spring Haiku

Spring, a great season!

Pretty flowers start to grow.

Then all beauty shows.

(Written at age 8)

Moon Haiku

The moon moves slightly

right across the big blue sky,

making the stars cry.

(Written at age 8)

Acrostic

Jelly and peanut butter sandwiches are the best.

Everybody who is nice is my friend.

No name is dull to me, and I love mine.

Never hate a creature, even the bee.

I really like geckos, and I have one as a pet.

Falling leaves I love to collect.

Everybody to me seems to very fine.

Rubies and diamonds are not as special as the true
pleasure of friends.

(Written at age 8)

Made in the USA
Charleston, SC
16 September 2016